# CHECK OUT OTHER TITLES BY THE CARTEL PUBLICATIONS

SHYT LIST 1
SHYT LIST 2
SHYT LIST 3
SHYT LIST 4
SHYT LIST 5
PITBULLS IN A SKIRT 1
PITBULLS IN A SKIRT 2
PITBULLS IN A SKIRT 3
POISON 1
POISON 2
VICTORIA'S SECRET
HELL RAZOR HONEYS 1
HELL RAZOR HONEYS 2
BLACK AND UGLY AS EVER
A HUSTLER'S SON 2
THE FACE THAT LAUNCHED A THOUSAND BULLETS
YEAR OF THE CRACKMOM
THE UNUSUAL SUSPECTS
MISS WAYNE AND THE QUEENS OF DC
LA FAMILIA DIVIDED
RAUNCHY
RAUNCHY 2: MAD'S LOVE
RAUNCHY 3: JAYDEN'S PASSION
REVERSED
QUITA'S DAYSCARE CENTER
QUITA'S DAYSCARE CENTER 2
DEAD HEADS
DRUNK & HOT GIRLS
THE END. HOW TO WRITE A BESTSELLING NOVEL IN 30 DAYS

WWW.THECARTELPUBLICATIONS.COM

What Up Fam,

This novel is full of nonstop action and adventure and teaches a great lesson. Always be careful what you wish for because you just might get it. These girls are a crazy ass mess and if you like messy situations, I know you'll love, "Drunk & Hot Girls".

Keeping in line with Cartel tradition, we would like to honor an author who's literary work we admire and moving forward we decided that we will not only pay homage to authors but go getters in life and business. In this letter, we would like to pay tribute to:

*Ray Lewis*

Ray Anthony Lewis is an American football linebacker who has played with the Baltimore Ravens from 1996 to the present. He is considered to be one of the best linebackers of all time. Ray Lewis is the heart and soul of the Baltimore Ravens football team. He is widely respected as a great linebacker and motivator and will be truly missed when he retires after the post NFL season ends in 2013. We at the Cartel Publications love you Ray Lewis and thank you for the great games!

Ok, I'm out, got work to do!

Much Love, Success and Happiness.

Charisse "C. Wash" Washington
Vice President
The Cartel Publications
www.thecartelpublications.com
www.twitter.com/cartelbooks
www.facebook.com/cartelcafeandbooksstore
www.facebook.com/publishercharissewashington
www.twitter.com/CWashVP
Follow us on Instagram @cartelpublications
Follow me on Instagram @publishercwash

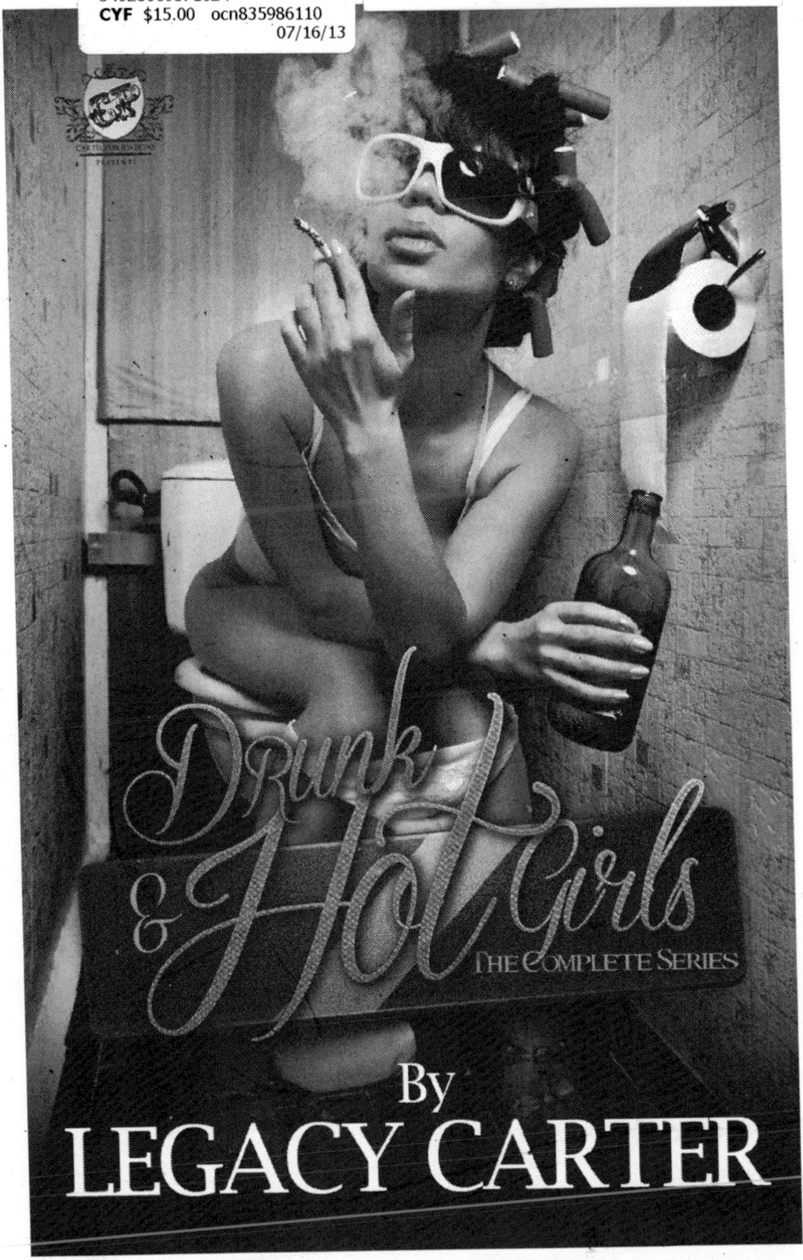
Drunk & Hot Girls
The Complete Series
By
LEGACY CARTER

PUBLISHER'S NOTE:
This book is a work of fiction. Names, characters, businesses, Organizations, places, events and incidents are the product of the Author's imagination or are used fictionally. Any resemblance of Actual persons, living or dead, events, or locales are entirely coincidental.

Library of Congress Control Number: 2013930810

ISBN 13: 978-0984993055

Cover Design: Davida Baldwin www.oddballdsgn.com
Editor: Advanced Editorial Services
Graphics: Davida Baldwin
www.thecartelpublications.com
First Edition

Printed in the United States of America

# Prologue

I wasn't always a drunk. Two weeks ago I couldn't even stand the smell of liquor. Can you believe that one chore for my mother, coupled with an unplanned car ride, would end up in me needing a drink just to survive?

"Just one taste, Porsche," Champagne told me. "It ain't like you can get hooked or nothing. This shit is like oil. It'll just loosen you up so that you can enjoy life a little. For goodness sake, Porsche…live a little."

Since the first time I allowed her dick smelling hands to pass me my first drink, my world has been turned upside down. As much as I want to, for your sake, I can't rush my story along. Besides, it's unfair for you to be entertained by my pain without hearing the entire story.

I gotta give you the first day it all started. You have to bare witness to my crazy ass story, and feel my pain. Maybe warn others to beware of shiny cars, and pretty faces.

When I'm done, only then will I tell you how I ended up here, in a shallow grave, probably for the rest of my young life.

# DAY ONE
# WET WEDNESDAY
## Chapter One

Why my mother couldn't get off of her boney ass, to go to the store herself is beyond me. The weatherman says it's 99 degrees but it feels more like 500. It's so hot outside that the red tank top I'm wearing is clinging to my back, because of my own sweat.

When I dig into the tiny pocket of the tight black shorts I'm wearing, I pull out a moist twenty-dollar bill. My mother wants me to use it to buy her a bottle of Passion Fruit Smirnoff vodka, from Eazy's Liquor store up the block. It's the only place that allows me to buy alcohol without a driver's license. I hate being seventeen.

When I see a pile of broken glass in front of me, I walk around it, because I'm not wearing my shoes. My gold sandals dangle in my hand, but they hurt my feet on the sides, so I don't wear them. They rub against my baby toes and make them sore.

"Hey, Twin," someone yells behind me. When I look back I see Chris' yellow Polo shirt. He's waving at me from the stoop of his apartment building. Fuck Chris black ass.

I let the nigga finger fuck me in the back of his mother's truck a few days ago for ten dollars. Instead of giving me my money, he gave me a McDonald's Happy Meal instead.

Talking about he'll get me later on the rest. I hate empty-ass niggas.

Instead of responding to him I continue on my way to the store. "I know you not still mad about that shit the other day," he yells at my back. "I got you on the rest, if you let me hit," he laughs.

He's trying to play me in front of everybody. So I spin around, throw my middle finger up and yell, "Fuck you, you broke ass nigga!"

"Suck my dick!" He yells back. "My shit smells better than your pussy." He laughed louder and when I look back I can see that his little crew is outside. I fucked all of them, so they better not even fake like they don't know what's up with my juicy. Every last one of them be on it when I come outside, and they by they self. But, in front of each other, they front. "Come on, Twin. I'm just fucking with you."

Since my mother moved us to Lavender Projects a year ago, in Washington, D.C., people around here always called me Twin. It didn't matter that I told them my name was Porsche Shakur. They called me what they want, and I got tired of telling them what my name was so I left them to it.

These niggas around here are so Monday. They do the same shit day after day, and I hate living around here. I need fun in my life.

*Dear God, please give me an adventure. Take me away from my mother, my boring school, and this neighborhood.*

All my mother wants to do is talk about how important school is, and drink vodka. If she's not drinking she's drawing sketches on blank sheets of paper. Sometimes I see her take the sketches out of the house, and she may come back with a little bit of money. But, she never gives none to me so I don't give a fuck.

I don't have any friends and at this point I would do anything to get away. It's the only thing I pray about everyday.

As I hold my mother's wet twenty-dollar bill in my hand, I try to think of a lie I can tell her to take the money, and spend it on myself. Maybe I can tell her I was kidnapped, and held at gunpoint for it. Maybe I can tell her that I was robbed, and raped.

I'm still thinking of a good lie, until I see the side of my uncle Todd's gray trench coat up the street. He's standing on the side of the liquor store, with this hands stuffed into his coat pockets. He's scratching his head and looking from left to right. It's hot as shit out here, and I can't understand why he would be wearing a coat.

Unlike my mother, my uncle gives me money every time I see him. It's usually at the first of the month though. My mother said it is because he draws Social Security. Normally he isn't out here. He lives in Virginia, so I figure he's coming to see my mother…his sister.

As I walk toward him I think about my uncle's past. Five years ago he was a famous gynecologist in D.C. But a few patients lied on him, and said he raped them while under the influence of anesthesia, and he lost his practice. That's sad, because my uncle is the best doctor ever.

"Hey, Uncle Todd," I yell tapping him on the shoulder. "I didn't know you were out here yet. Why didn't you call me?"

He turns around, pulls his coat closed, and looks at me. He smiles brightly and hugs me tightly. My sandals smack against his back. His thick beard rubs up against my forehead as he rocks me in his arms. I can smell the cigarettes on his skin, but I don't mind a bit. I love him so much.

"Hey, Porsche,' he says as he rocks me in his strong arms. "I didn't know you were out here." He pulls me closer to him. "What you doing out here looking all pretty and stuff? You gonna make me fuck these young niggas up out here trying to get at you."

I think about my body. I'm short, about five-five, and light skin. Although I got big titties, and a fat ass, I'm still a little chubby, especially around the waist. Niggas tell me all the time that my body is still right, but I never believe them. So when he tells me I'm pretty, it makes me love him more.

"Ain't nobody checking for me," I say talking into his musty chest. "Not boys anyway."

"Then they are fools," he says holding me tighter.

Our bodies meshed together are making me hotter. I'm sweating more. So when he finally lets me go, I sigh in relief. Finally I can breathe. "Thanks, unc." I smile up at him. "What you doing out here?"

His eyes widen. "Why, who said something?"

I laugh at him. He's weird at times, but I think it's funny. "Nobody," I giggle. "I was just on my way to the store for mama. But, she only gave me enough cash for her vodka." I look up at him. "You got any money on you I can borrow?"

He laughs at me, digs into his pocket and pulls out a five-dollar bill. He doesn't give it to me just yet. "You gotta give me another hug first." He opens his arms. "So bring it in."

I step back into his embrace. He pulls me closer to him, and his hands run over my round ass. I'm just about to ask him what he's doing when through the space under his arm I see a dude holding a silver baseball bat. The sun shining on the bat makes it look platinum. To his right is a girl wearing a pink short set, and, behind them were five other teenagers.

"There he is right there," the girl in the pink shorts, says pointing at my uncle with what looks like a knife.

My uncle pushes away from me, and before I knew it the crowd is upon us. The teenager with the bat said, "You sure this is him?" He looks down at Pink Shorts.

I stand behind my uncle, not sure what is going on.

"Yeah, that's him. I was going to this store right here to buy me a strawberry soda, when he pulled out his dick, and told me to touch it."

My eyes widen. "Stop lying," I yell at her. "My uncle wouldn't do nothing like that."

Before I know it, Mr. Bat is busting my uncle in his head with the bat. I see red blood splatter everywhere and all on my black shorts. Then outta no where Pink Shorts says, "And that's his niece. Let's beat her ass too."

I was about to run for my life when a beautiful black E-Class Benz pulled up on the curb and stopped on the side of me. "Come on in, Twin," says Champagne, one of the flyest girls in my neighborhood. "And, make it quick before they kill you out here."

# Chapter Two

I'm rubbing my hands over the butter soft chestnut colored leather in the expensive Benz. I never been in a car like this before.

"Twin, why do you smell like onions?" Champagne asks me. She's in the backseat with me.

When I look over at Champagne she's frowning at me. My eyes roll over her long black weave, her light skin face and the diamond rings on her fingers. She looks like she just stepped out of a music video. I wonder how she gets her makeup so pretty, and where she found the orange colored lipstick she's wearing.

"My name is, Porsche," I say softly. "I don't know why people keep calling me Twin."

"You still haven't answered the question," she reaches into her black Louis Vuitton bag and pulls out a liquor flask. It has crystals all over it, and looks very expensive too. She lifts it to her lips, pours some inside of her mouth and says, "Want some?"

"I don't drink," I say remembering how funky my mother's throw up smells when she drinks too much. "I'm good. Thanks anyway."

"Why do you smell like onions?" She twists the cap back on and places it back into her purse.

I lift up my right arm and sniff. I raise my lift arm and sniff. I don't smell anything. "My underarms smell fine to me."

"Well maybe it's your pussy instead," she says. "Either way you need to handle business when you out in these streets."

Embarrassed, I look up at the driver. He's wearing a black and white Brooklyn Nets cap. He looks about twenty-eight years old. But, more importantly, he doesn't appear to be listening to me.

"I didn't get a chance to take a bath today," I clear my throat. "I had to go to the store for my mother, and was going to take a bath when I got back."

"A real bitch doesn't leave the house without washing her bank," she points at me with her black and gold colored nail. "That's rule number one in Real Bitch-ism."

"My bank?" I don't know what she means.

She shakes her head, and I feel so stupid. "Your bank is your pussy. As long as you got a wet and clean one, you will never go broke. Some bitches don't realize it and they miss out on they full worth, and earning potential. But I don't. Take care of your pussy, and you shouldn't have a care in the world."

I think about what she said. My mother taught me I should excel in school, and think about what career I wanted in life. She never told me about the importance of my pussy. Suddenly I feel like she cheated me on a life lesson.

"What happened back there," she says nodding her head toward the back window. "With Touching Todd?"

"Touching Todd?" I lean in to her. "What you mean?"

She laughs so hard she grips her stomach. "Damn, girl. You don't know shit do you? Do you ever get out of the house?"

I shrug.

"Touching Todd is your uncle. He done showed his dick to every girl on the block. Even I seen that mothafucka before. I will give him one thing, he is packing."

When the car swerves Champagne looks up at the driver and places her hand on his shoulder. He gets the car under control.

"My uncle not like that," I say. "He don't show people his dick."

"Twin, you not gonna tell me that-that man has never touched you before," she slaps my red legs. "As thick as you are?" She shakes her head from left to right. "Naw, he stepped to this before didn't he? I know it. He had to get a taste of this pussy."

I'm mad at what she saying about my uncle. Plus I remember what he just did to me at the store, by touching my ass. I try to put what he did out of my mind.

Where is she taking me? I'm so bored at home that I keep my mouth closed, and go along for the ride. The other fucked up part is that I don't own a cell phone. So if something happened I wouldn't be able to call for help.

"You not mad at what I said are you?" She asks me as the driver makes a left into a parking lot. "If me and you gonna be cool, I believe in keeping shit real."

When she says me, and her are going to be cool it takes everything in me not to jump up and down off of the windows in this car. I would love to hang out with somebody like her. When I see we are driving into the parking lot of the H-Street Motel, my heart thumps wildly.

I look at Champagne and say, "I'm not fucking nobody in there. Just so you know."

Champagne looks at the driver, and they both break out into heavy laughter. The driver stops laughing after he parks, but it takes Champagne a minute longer to stop completely. "Don't flatter yourself, sweetheart. With the way that pussy is pounding right now, you ain't gotta worry about me, or anybody I know wanting to fuck you. So relax. You good."

Why do I feel so dumb being around her? It's like she doesn't like me, but wants me around for some reason. What could I possibly have that she would want anyway? I don't got no money. Apparently my pussy is not up to par, so what she need with me? As I brush my hand over my messy ponytail, I wait until she opens the car door.

"Get out," she tells me. "We about to go inside."

I slide my shoes on my feet. I ease out, and follow her to the driver's side window. She digs into her pocket, and hands him something quickly. I can't see what it is, but the driver stuffs it into his pocket. From where I stand, I see a bunch of cut off pieces of paper in the passenger seat. They have different things written on them, but I can't read them from where I am.

After she finishes with him she says, "Let's go upstairs."

We walk up the motel steps. Just like I thought, the sandals are rubbing against my baby toes making it hard to walk straight.

"Your shoes too tight or something?" She asks me looking at my feet.

"No, they just rub against my toes."

She laughs at me. "Then it means they too tight," she shakes her head. "What size shoes you wear?"

"Seven and a half."

"On cheap shoes you might have to go a size up or down. Keep that in mind for future reference."

I feel dumb again. Maybe I should just shut up. I follow her to room number 566. When she opens the door, I see twin beds. There are two white boxes of Chinese food on the table, and a brown bag. I can tell she's been in the room already. Champagne throws her purse on the table, and takes off her silver shoes. They're red at the bottom and I figure they them rich shoes girls like her be wearing.

"Get comfortable," she tells me after taking the flask from her purse and drinking the liquor again.

I take my shoes off, and sit on the edge of the bed.

"Not that one," she frowns and points at another bed. "Use the other bed instead."

I step on my sandals on the way to the other bed, closer to the window. I take a seat. I watch her from behind. Champagne's ass is so big I don't understand why she doesn't fall back. And her waist is as small as a pole.

She goes through her purse, and pulls out a stack of money. It's more money than I've ever seen in my life. She walks up to me, and gives me a one hundred dollar bill. I reluctantly take it out of her hand. My heart is beating so fast again. I never held this much money in my hands before.

I look up at her. "What I gotta do for this?"

"Go in that bathroom, and wash your funky ass," she laughs. "Let's start there."

I stuff the money in my pocket with my mother's twenty-dollar bill. I stand up and walk to the bathroom. Something tells me I should get as far away from her as possible, but I don't want to go. I turn the water on, and wash my body real good. I scrubbed myself so hard my skin felt sore. I didn't want Champagne to have to say anything else about how I smell later.

When I was done washing up, I dry my body, and use the deodorant on the sink. Then I sprayed the Chanel No. 5 perfume on my skin that was also on the bathroom sink. I never smelled so beautiful before. When I'm done I grab my white underwear on the floor and put them back on. Then I put on my black shorts and my red top. When I'm dressed I walk out of the bathroom.

Her eyes widen. "What the fuck?" She looks at my clothes. "Why would you put on the same shit that stank earlier?"

"What am I going to wear? I didn't bring nothing else."

She points at my bed. "That right there." She pauses. "Now take that shit off, and put on the new clothes. Before you have to wash up again. Damn, girl. Use your head."

I pick up the jeans first. The label says *True Religion.* I never heard of these kind of jeans before. I grab the pink top and recognize the green Polo horse on it. She even had a pair of white silk panties for me with a tag inside of them. They were new. "Where did you get these clothes?"

"A real bitch keeps a fresh pair of clothes on her at all times. That's Real-Bitch-ism rule number two."

I take the clothes to the bathroom, and get dressed. They fit my body perfectly, and since Champagne is a different size than me, I wonder who they belong too. I take the money from my shorts, and stuff the one hundred and twenty dollars in my jean pocket. When I'm dressed I come back out, and can smell a hot iron. When I walk further into the bedroom I see a tall girl standing behind a chair.

"Come over here," she tells me. "I need to hook that head up."

I look at Champagne. It's not my birthday so all of the special treatment I'm receiving feels so weird. I take a seat in front of the hairdresser, and she takes my ponytail out and does my hair. Champagne comes in front of me and slides a pair of black Michael Kors snakeskin tennis shoes on my feet. They are so cute.

When my hair is done, the girl pulls out a large black bag. When she pushes it out, I see a rack of lipsticks and eye shadow. She wipes my face with something, and then does my makeup. She even gives me eyelashes and I can't wait to see what I look like in the mirror.

An hour later, I look in the mirror, and cry. I've never looked so pretty in all of my life. My brown hair is now chopped into a cute little bob. And, every time I move my head it shakes. I feel so beautiful.

I look at the hairdresser and say, "Thank you. I love it."

She ignores me and holds out her hand. When I look at Champagne she nods. I understand now. They want the money Champagne gave me earlier. I give her the one hundred dollars and she walks out the door. Had I known my money would've been used on this I would not have given it to her.

But when I look at how pretty I look again in the mirror, I don't care. I can't wait until the people in my neighborhood see me like this. "So what we gonna do now?"

The moment I ask there is a knock at the door. When Champagne goes and opens it, there is a big fat girl on the other side. She's wearing a yellow shirt with a red clown on the front and she looks angry. Especially when Champagne points to me and says, "That's the girl you looking for right there."

# Chapter Three

As I look at Champagne's back while she talks to the girl at the door I was confused. How can I be the person she's looking for when I don't even know her?

"Nita, trust me, we gonna find Brillo," Champagne says. "If anything we need Crystal because she was the one who saw him get jacked."

The girl I now knew as Nita scratched inside one of the rows of her braids, before scratching her hairy chin. "How come I don't believe shit you say, Champagne? Everybody knows you a drunk bitch. How I know you not trying to get over on me and my brother Axe?"

"Because I ain't got no reason to lie," Champagne responds.

Nita walks up to me. I can smell a strong scent of cigarettes steaming off of her skin. She stands in front of me for a second and observes me. I can't read her facial expression. I can feel sweat rolling from under my arms, and down the side of my stomach. Thank God I just took a shower and put on fresh deodorant.

"Tell me what happened?" She asks me.

What can I say to her? I don't know what the fuck she's talking about. I don't even know what's going on. Why am I even here? One minute I was walking down the street to get my mother's vodka, and the next minute I was being cleaned up, and asked to give a story I didn't know.

Instead of answering her right away I said, "I gotta go to the bathroom. I'll be right back." Before she could respond I take off toward the bathroom and lock the door behind me. I sit on the toilet and look at the closed door. I'm trying to find out how to get out of here, but can't think of any way. There are no windows in the bathroom.

From inside the bathroom I hear Nita say, "Something is up here. Why the fuck she run in the bathroom like that?"

"She had to use the bathroom," Champagne says to her.

"I don't believe what the fuck you saying to me, drunk bitch. If she saw what happened to Brillo, how come she didn't just come out and say it?"

"Nita, I'm not trying to go at you like that, but you are kind of scary. Maybe she was intimidated. But, I can tell you what happened in that white Honda myself."

"Shut up, bitch! I don't want you to tell me. You said the girl knows so I'll wait to hear what she has to say. I got a feeling you gonna say whatever you can to clear your own name."

Suddenly I have to really use the bathroom. But, when I move to handle business, there is a bang at the door.

"What you doing in there, Crystal?" Nita asks banging on the door. "You ain't fall in did you?"

"Who the fuck is Crystal?" I ask.

Silence.

"What you just say?" She asks at the door.

"I said—,"

"Crystal, stop fucking around with Nita," Champagne laughs. "You gonna make this girl think you serious."

"Who the fuck is that bitch in there?" Nita asks. "She not Brillo's girl is she?"

"I told you," Champagne responds. "She's Crystal, Brillo's girlfriend."

"Show me a picture," she says. "I want to see a picture of her and Brillo together right now. Because, I can't remember what she looks like."

"I don't have one," Champagne laughs. "What I look like carrying a picture of my friend and her boyfriend in my phone?"

"You think this is a joke don't you?" Nita says. "You really think I won't go off in this bitch." She pauses. "Well if you do you really don't know me. I don't give a fuck about either one of you bitches. The only thing me and Axe care about is Brillo and what happened last night. Mothafuckas around the city hollering about Crystal was dead, and then you telling me she's alive, and here. But when I try to talk to shorty in the bathroom, she acts like she don't know what's going on."

I was looking at the bathroom door like it was a movie. More like a horror movie. My worst fear was that at any minute, the door would come crashing in. My fears seemed realer when she banged on the door again.

"Come out here," she yells at me. "Right now! I'm not fucking around with you."

"I'm almost—"

Before I could give her a response there was a loud blast by the door nob. Now there's a huge hole. I can see them on the other side. I held my heart, because I wasn't expecting her to shoot the door. Nita stomps into the bathroom, pulls me off of the toilet by my hair and drags me into the bedroom. Once I was there she threw me on the floor and looked down at me.

While the gun was pointed at me she says, "Show me a picture of Brillo in your phone."

"I don't have a cell phone," I say trying not to pass out.

"How the fuck you don't have a cell phone when everybody knows what you, Champagne, and Marcy be into?"

I look at her clenched fist. "What do you mean?" I ask hoping she won't hit me.

"Everybody know that you, Champagne, and that bitch Marcy are a bunch of drunk whores who will do anything for money. So it doesn't make sense to me unless you ain't Crystal."

I know I'm not Crystal, but nobody wants to listen. When I look at Champagne she looks like she wants to cry. Something tells me to tell her who I am, and where Champagne picked me up. I've never been involved in anything like this before and I feel like I'm in over my head. So I go with the story.

"I am Crystal," I say.

I can hear Champagne exhale. "You see, Nita," Champagne says. "Now let the girl up. You been too serious and you gonna scare her off. Don't forget that she's the only one who can identify the niggas who took Brillo."

"Not so fast, drunk," Nita pulls out her phone and dials a number. I look at the door, and contemplate running for it to save my own life. Nita must've heard my thoughts because she places her foot on my chest and presses down. "Bitch, if you move for that door I'll splatter your shit all over this room. I'm talking about closed casket shit all the way."

I swallow hard. "I'm not going anywhere," I whisper.

"I didn't think so," she responds.

As she holds the phone to her ear I look at Champagne. At first Champagne looks sorry for me, and then she walks to her purse, takes out the crystal flask and drinks some of whatever's inside. She goes to the paper bag on the table, pulls out a new bottle of Smirnoff vodka. She twists the top off, and pours it down her throat.

I'm still focusing on Champagne until I hear Nita say, "Janice, remember we threw Brillo that birthday party last year?" She pauses. "Yeah that's the one." She takes her foot off my chest and walks a few feet over…next to the bathroom door. "Well I need you to send me that picture. The one of Brillo and his girlfriend. You know, the freak bitch I can't stand. I think she was eating a hot dog and he was hugging her from behind." She looks over at me. I need to see about something." She pauses again. "I know you heard that she was dead, but apparently she's back to life, because I'm staring at her right now."

I get up off the floor and sit on the edge of my bed. When Champagne looks at me I look at Nita. When I see Nita is still on the call I whisper to Champagne, "What am I gonna do now?"

She places her finger over her lips and says, "Shhh."

I know now that she cares more about herself than she does me. I gotta get out of here. I gotta get out of here, and I gotta do it now. Because, once that picture comes, and Nita sees that it isn't me, she's going to kill me.

In a surprising turn of events Nita goes into the bathroom to talk on the phone. And, when she does, I make a run for the door. It seems like it takes me forever to get there. But, once I do, I turn the doorknob, pull it open and dash down the hall.

"Don't go, Crystal," Champagne yells behind me. "She gonna kill us."

I ignore her. I haven't been running for that long, but my chest is already hard. Maybe it's because of the heart murmur I was born with. Suddenly I don't have any energy.

Once I reach the stairs, instead of running down them, I collapse right at the top step.

When I come to I'm laying on the floor with my hands tied behind my back. Now there's another girl in the room with us. She's skinny, with blue curly hair and fat lips. She's chewing a wad of pink gum. I know it because her mouth keeps opening wide every time she chews, and pops a bubble.

"So what do you think, Janice?" Nita says looking at me while pointing the gun in my direction. "Is this Brillo's girlfriend or not? Because, after that stunt she just pulled, if she ain't his bitch, she's as good as dead."

Janice walks closer to me, while popping gum. When she's standing over top of me, she gets down on all fours. She grabs my cheeks, and turns my head from left to right. Then she digs into her jean pocket and pulls out an iPhone.

I close my eyes and say the Lord's Prayer. My mother makes me say it every night before I go to bed, so I know it by heart. It doesn't matter that I'm almost eighteen. It also doesn't matter that I think my mother's a hypocrite, since she drinks everyday. All that matters to her is that I talk to God. So, I do it now.

Right before I'm about to start Janice says, "This the same girl. She just looks a little browner. If this ain't her they could be identical twins." She hands Nita the phone. "See."

I look at the picture before she hands it to Nita. I don't see the girl but I see Brillo. He's so cute. The kind of boy who I would like, but who never likes me back. Nita examines the picture and looks at my face.

I wonder if Crystal is the reason everybody in my neighborhood calls me twin.

She looks at the picture, and looks at me again. "Damn, I guess this really is you." She gives Janice back the phone. "Now tell me why you were covered in a lot of blood last night, and Brillo not answering the phone for his family?"

I'm in over my head. I need some help. So I take a few quick breaths and say, "He was…I was…I mean…he was taking me to get something to eat," I look at Champagne who nods her head, and smiles. I must be doing good so far. "And we were sitting at the light. Before, he could pull off two dudes jumped out, and pulled their guns out." I look at Champagne again. She's still smiling. Nita stands in front of her and I can't see Champagne anymore.

"Brillo, tried to defend me, but everything moved so fast," I continue. "The next thing I know, they're taking

Brillo at gunpoint. But, Brillo was able to hit one of them in the face, which is how I got blood all over me. Maybe people thought I died, because of that."

Nita looked down at me as if she didn't believe me. But, how can I blame her when I didn't even believe myself.

"So you're telling me that they took Brillo but you got away?"

"He told me to get out of there. But, I didn't want to leave him. And then he started screaming at me. So what was I to do? I ran as fast as I could."

Nita took a look at Champagne and frowned. She walks over to her and places her hand around her throat. With the other hand she points in her face. "If my little brother is not back here by midnight I'm killing you," she looks at me, "and you, and anybody you love. Now that's just what I'm going to do. There's no telling what Axe will do if you don't find him."

Champagne took a swig of her vodka, wiped her mouth with the back of her hand, and says, "don't worry about it. Brillo will be back here and safe at midnight."

"For your sake you better hope that's true," Nita says. "Find him ASAP, or the deal is off."

# Chapter Four

This time I'm sitting in the backseat of the Benz alone. Champagne is in the front passenger seat, and to tell you the truth I'm grateful. Because I have my hands stuffed between my legs trying to convince myself I don't have to pee. I know it's stupid, but I'm afraid to ask them to stop somewhere so I can use the bathroom. Things seem so tense now since we left the motel room.

"Champagne, where are we going now?" I ask her. "Because is getting, late and I really have to get home. My mother is probably worried about me."

She turns around and looks at me. She seems irritated. And, I feel like a kid. "After what just happened back in that motel, you really need to chill, and shut the fuck up." She turns back around, and folds her arms over her breasts. "I don't have time for your shit right now."

I lean back in my seat, and cry. For some reason I wish my mother was here. That's crazy, because before this moment, my mother and I didn't get along. I wonder if she's looking for me, and if she'll call the police if I'm not home within a few more hours. I guess the worst part about all of this is that I don't know what's going on. And, Champagne doesn't seem to want to help me figure it all out.

When I look straight ahead I can feel the dude who hasn't said anything to me since he first picked me up, staring at me through the rearview mirror. I wonder why he doesn't talk, and if he approves of what Champagne is doing to me.

As I’m sitting here in the backseat, I'm thinking about the worst-case scenario. If I had to pretend to be Crystal, then it probably means that she's dead. And if she is dead then it probably means they killed her. Finally I know what I have to do. Even if they tell me I'm not a hostage, which nobody has yet, I still have to get as far away from her and this man as possible.

So I look at Champagne, and then I look at the man, and they appear to be looking out ahead of them. Toward the road. So I look down to my left, and run my hand over the door handle. The moment we come to a light, I'm going to open this bitch, and make a run for it. I just hope I'm able to get away, before they do to me what I think they did to Crystal, murder me in cold blood.

The moment I think about my escape, I see the light ahead of me turn yellow. I probably look so crazy in the backseat of this car with one hand on the door and the other stuck between my legs, while I’m hyperventilating. When he slows the car up, and comes to a light, I'm about to pull it, when Champagne starts talking to me.

"You hungry back there?" She asks as she looks into my eyes. "And why the fuck are you sweating so hard? You not on cocaine are you? Because, I don’t fuck with that shit." Her eyes roll over my hand, which is holding the door handle. Her attitude changes now.

"Yes, I…can…probably eat something."

"That's good, because were thinking about stopping somewhere in a minute," she says as her eyes maintain their focus on the door handle, and my shaky fingers. "I haven't eaten all day."

"Oh…me either. I'm so hungry now I can eat anything," I say. I release the door handle and put my hand in my lap, with the other one. "Where were you thinking about stopping?"

"I'm not sure yet, but I can't let you do what you are about to do, Porsche," she says changing the subject. "At least not right now anyway."

I smile again, although I feel stupid now. "I don't know what you're talking about. Do what?"

"Don't play dumb with me, bitch. If there's one thing I hate it somebody making a fool out of me. So if you trying to make me angry, you are doing a good job."

"I wasn't trying to do that," I say shivering. "But can I ask you something?"

"What is it?" She turns back around and folds her arms over her breasts again. "Because I don't like a bunch of questions either."

I swallow and say, "Can I leave whenever I want to? Because it feels like I can’t go home."

She turns back around, smiles at me and says, "Of course you can." The grin on her face looks fake. Like one of the women in my mother's paintings. "Why would you even ask me some shit like that? I’m not about handcuffing anybody. So sit back and relax. I got you."

I don't want to rock the boat right now. So instead of telling her that the way she looks at me creeps me out, and how for the first time I can remember I want to see my mother's face again I say, "No reason I guess."

Before I know it we pull up at an IHOP restaurant. The man parks the car, and Champagne slides out first. I open my car door, and approach her as she walks to the driver side. But the moment I come behind her, she whips her head around and says, "Go the fuck in the restaurant! Damn! What you trying to do, listen to my personal conversation or something?" She looks evil. More evil than she looked a few minutes ago.

I take two steps back and say, "I'll wait for you inside."

I turned to run away when I feel a hard yank on my wrist. When I look down at my arm I see Champagne's sparkly black nails digging into the flesh of my arm. When I look into her eyes she says, "If you try to run I will hurt you. And, it will be bad too." And then she smiles and says, "Now go find us a table and get whatever you want to eat." She places her hand over her chest. "It's on me."

I don't even know I'm crying, until I can't see anymore because my vision is blurred. I rush into the restaurant, and am met by a hostess. She's grinning from ear to ear. I hate when people are extra nice when I'm mad at the world.

"How many guests?" She asks me.

I don't know if the man is coming inside to eat too so I say, "Three."

She grabs three menus, and walks me to a section in the back of the restaurant. "Your waitress will be here in a moment," she says before dropping me off at my table, slapping the menus on top of it, and walking back to the front.

I place my hands on the brown table in front of me. I look around the restaurant. When I see two cops walk in, I'm tempted to tell them that I'm being held against my will. I'm just about to get up to approach them when I think about what they may ask me. They'll probably ask questions like, *did they point a gun at you?* The only person who held a gun on me was Nita, Brillo's sister. Still I couldn't help but feel that this was my only hope. I must tell them I need help.

I was just about to get up when Champagne walks into the restaurant with the man. Champagne looks at the officers, and the man, and back at me. She switches all the way to the table, and sits directly in front of me. The man sits next to her. They are on the opposite side of the table. I feel like I'm about to be interrogated.

For a moment we just stare at each other. For some reason, silence scares me more than words themselves. Whenever my mother used to get mad at me, and not talk to me for days, I remember it being some of the loneliest times of my life. But, at least I knew where my mother was coming from. I don't know Champagne at all. I don't know what she's capable of. I used to think she was the coolest person, but now I think she's the meanest person I've ever met in my life. Outside of Nita.

"So have you decided which you want to eat yet?" Champagne asks me.

I swallow and say, "Pancakes and eggs probably."

"Girl, I'm treating and that's the only thing you're going to eat? After the day we had today if I were you I would eat me out of house and home," she raises the menu and lifts it to her face. "Well me and him eating good today."

"I guess I'm not as hungry as I thought I was," I say.

The waitress eventually takes our orders. I look at the police officers take a seat. They sit two booths down from us. If I talk in a regular tone they could probably hear everything I say. And when I look back at Champagne she is staring directly into my eyes. It's like she can read my mind, and know that I'm about to say something to the police.

"Don't be stupid, Porsche. Please don't make him do something to you that wasn't planned," she says looking at the man, and then back at me.

When I look at the man he's glaring at me. As if I'd just stolen something from him. To cut his stare I raise the menu to cover my eyes. I'm not looking at anything in particular. It's dawning on me that the only way I'm going to get away from her is if she lets me.

When the food comes I'm surprised that I'm as hungry as I am. I ate all of my pancakes, which I normally never do, and ordered three glasses of orange juice. It's not until then that I realize I hadn't gone to the bathroom yet. Thoughts of escaping play around in my mind, and I try to push them out. I figure if I play along this will all be over soon.

I look at Champagne and say, "What happened to Crystal?"

Champagne puts her glass of water down and says, "Do you really want to know?"

I think I want to but the way she says it has me doubting myself. "Well is she at least alive? Can you tell me that?"

She doesn't say anything to me. Just more of that crazy silence she's been giving me all day. I grab my orange juice and shake the ice up that's in the bottom of my glass. "What about Brillo? Is he still alive?"

She looks at the man and then back at me. "Do you really want to know, Porsche? Because with answers come great responsibility. And, with great responsibility comes greater risks. Now I have no problem telling you everything you want to know. Just be clear that if I do, if something happens the knowledge you have could mean your life. Do you want to ask those same questions again?"

I swallow, and shake my head rapidly from left to right. I feel dizzy now. "No that's okay. I'm good."

She laughs and says, "I figured you'd think that way." She looks at the gold Bulova watch on her arm. Her eyes widen and she says to the man, "Oh shit! My God daughter's birthday party is going on now. We have to get over there!" She throws some money on the table for the bill, and they stand up. I stand up too, just not as fast.

As I move in the direction of the police officers I decide I want to tell them I'm being held captive anyway. Even if it means my life. I walk slower now so that I can put some space between me and Champagne.

When I'm inches away from the police's table, suddenly the man comes back into the restaurant, and wraps his arms around my waist. We are right in front of the police's table now, and my voice feels trapped in my throat. The man presses his lips upon mine, stuffs his stiff tongue into my mouth. His mouth tastes nasty. Like he smokes too many cigarettes.

When he separates the policemen smile at us and shake their heads. "Isn't that cute…love birds."

The man whisks me out of the restaurant and throws me into the car. Once inside Champagne is already there with an attitude. "Just one more time, Porsche. Just do what you just did once more. And, I'll forget how important you are to me. Do you understand?"

I nod my head up and down quickly. My neck feels loose now. Like it's not screwed on anymore.

"Good. Because that's my last time talking to you."

I throw myself in the backseat and cry silently. I hate both of them so much, but I know they don't care.

Five minutes later we're standing outside of the door of a large house in Washington DC. Champagne has in her hand a large pink and silver gift bag that she got from the trunk of the Benz. She seems overly excited, and I figure who ever this house belongs to, the people inside are important to her. But, the moment someone opens the door, and hug her, their focus seems to be glued on me.

The woman's jaw drops. "Oh my God," she screams pointing at me. "I thought Crystal was dead!"

# Chapter Five

The pink balloon that is tied on the lamp next to me keeps hitting me in the side of my head. I don't want to be here. I want to go home.

I'm not alone on this couch. But, I don't know the person next to me. It's a girl about my age give or take a day or two. She's looking at me. Then again everyone at this party keeps looking at me. To hear them tell it I'm not supposed to be alive. Maybe it is a dream. Maybe I am dead. I have to remember that they all think I'm Crystal.

As I look out into the party from this couch, I see a lot of happy faces. Even Champagne who hasn't said a nice thing to me since she met me, seems to be enjoying herself right now. When we first got here she gave the gift to a seven-year-old little girl wearing an orange and blue dress. Since no one bothered to introduce me to her I figure it's the little girl's birthday.

Now Champagne is hugging an older woman with a white colorful shirt, and baggy black jeans. I think she's her mother. It's not like anybody told me that either. I just recognize the look in her eyes as she looks at Champagne. My mother used to look at me the same way before she became an alcoholic. And, my daddy left.

A girl about 12 years old wearing a dirty white T-shirt stained with too much ice cream approaches me. Once she's in my breathing space I can smell candy on her skin. It's like she bathed in chocolate.

She points a long finger in my face and says, "I thought you suppose to be dead. At least that's what my mommy said."

I don't know what to say to her. Mainly because I'm not sure what I'm supposed to say to anybody. "If I were dead I wouldn't be here now would I? So your mother is a liar." I probably should not of said that but so what. I'm frustrated right now.

The little girl frowns. "Well why you mad at me? I didn't do nothing to you."

I sigh. "Look…all I want to be is left alone," I say focusing on the balloon. "This is a party, go enjoy yourself, and play with other kids."

"What heaven be like?" She asks tugging the bottom of her shirt. "Is it big and pretty?"

How the fuck would I know that? I want her to leave me alone, and get up out of my face. But, when I look around the party, for a place to run away from her, I can't find a safe space. Everyone has the same look on their face. They want to know why I'm here. They want to know why I'm alive.

Instead of walking away, I decide to stay right here on this couch. I turn my body so that the side of my arm is facing her direction. Maybe she'll leave me alone now.

"You want some cake?" She asks me.

I don't respond. When from the corner of my eye I see her walk away, I'm relieved. That is until Champagne comes over and sits next to me. She has a cup in her hand. And, I'm sure it's more liquor. She's an even bigger drunk than my mother.

"Why you look so sad?" Champagne asks me. "This is a party, you should be enjoying yourself. We got food, drinks and even smoke. What you want? I'll have somebody get it for you."

"I told you I don't drink alcohol. Now when are you going to take me home? I'm tired of being here. I'm tired of being around you, and these people I don't know."

Suddenly I feel strong, because of the amount of people in the house. I figure she won't hurt me if so many people witness it.

Champagne looks around the party, and lifts the clear plastic cup to her red lips. "I'm glad you're feeling yourself right now. But, you need to know that these are my family members, not yours. And, every last one of them will kill you if I give the word. You sure you want to get fly on me again?"

I look out into the party. I see kids, elderly people, teenagers, couples and when I look closer, a few killers. I believe her right away. "I'm not trying to get fly. I just want to go home. I don't like people thinking I'm dead when I'm alive. And, I don't like pretending to be somebody that I'm not. Somebody I don't even know."

"And I told you I'll let you go but not right now. And, since I control the show and not you, you'll have to deal with it. Okay?"

When I see the lady that I think is her mother approach us with the colorful shirt, I wonder why the woman seems so scared all of a sudden. Like she has some bad news, and she's coming to question Champagne about it.

"Champagne, what's this I hear about Brillo being missing? And where is Crystal?"

I'm so caught up in this drama that I was about to say here I am. I'm Crystal. But, her mother doesn't even look my way. It's like she knows I'm not the real Crystal. Maybe she's smarter than the rest of the people at this party.

"Mom, please don't worry about it," she says sipping her drink. "I got this, and everything is going to be okay. I'm a big girl now. And, you just have to trust me."

"Fuck being a big girl," her mother says. "I don't care how old you are you going to always be my daughter," she yells. "Slow your roll when you're talking to me. I'm your mother you're not mine."

I know this is serious, but Champagne has gotten on my nerves all day today. And, to tell you the truth it's kind of refreshing to hear her get hers for a change. So I just sit back, and wait for what Champagne has to say next.

"Mom, I know I'm your daughter. But, you worrying about shit that you don't have to worry about."

"So you're telling me that what I'm hearing is untrue? Crystal and Brillo aren't missing?"

"Yes there's a situation going on with Brillo and Crystal. But, it's nothing I can't handle myself."

Her mother frowns. "Does that Marcy bitch have anything to do with this? Because I told you a long time ago that you have to leave her alone. The two of you together are nothing but trouble. I mean, why do you insist on having this girl in your life is beyond me. You two aren't in a sexual relationship are you?"

"Mom, no," she yells.

"Then what is it about Marcy that you can't seem to stay away from?"

Champagne looks over at me. I guess to see if I was listening to her conversation. Of course I was. What else am I going to do? I'm bored out of my mind. But, when I see the look she gives me, I turn around and focus on the balloon instead. I tap it a few times and watch it bounce back and forth.

"Mom, Marcy has been my friend since I was in high school—"

"I don't give a fuck! It's because of that girl that you have an alcohol problem. Don't you see that you can't even go a day without drinking?" She takes the cup from Champagne's hand. "Isn't it apparent to you that you have a problem? Because it's apparent to everybody else. At the rate you and your friends are going, if Crystal is not dead then she's going to be. And, that goes for you, and anybody else you have in your life."

"Mom, I can't believe you're doing this in front of my company right now," Champagne says.

I wonder if she's talking about me, because, I'm far from company. I'm just some girl she picked up off the street, and won't let go.

"Champagne, it's time to get your life together. And it's time to do that now. Before somebody else gets hurt."

I wonder who else got hurt to begin with. Was it some strange girl like me that she picked up off the street? Who accepted a ride from a stranger, when all she wanted was to get home safe? Had my uncle not violated somebody's child in my neighborhood, I wouldn't be involved in any of this shit.

"Mom, can you at least tell me where this is coming from? It's like you hitting me with all of this shit out of nowhere. And at my goddaughter's birthday party too. This not right, mom."

"Well you're getting all of this now because I hardly ever see you anymore. One of these days something is going to happen to me, and you are going to regret how you're treating me right now. But, until that time comes, I want to do all I can to try to get you back on the right track. Now I'm telling you all of this right now, because word on the street is that Axe cannot find his brother. They said you were the last one with him. That's why I'm coming at you like this. My friend just called me on the phone and told me. Now do you know where he is or not?"

Champagne looks at me again, and I catch her glance. I didn't even know I was looking at them again. When I turn around to the balloon, it pops in my face, and makes a loud noise. I jump up and the man who drove us here reaches for his weapon and rushes over in our direction.

Champagne jumps up and grabs his hand that's about to pull out the weapon. It looks like he was coming for me.

"It's cool," Champagne tells him. "Everything is cool, Dragon. Relax."

The man I now know as Dragon releases the hold of his weapon and pulls down his shirt. "Now you watch Porsche," Champagne says to him. "I'm gonna go talk to ma in private."

"I can't believe you're still dealing with this no good ass nigga either," her mother says looking at Dragon.

"Mom, please stop," Champagne says. "Come with me over here. So we can talk in private."

When Champagne leaves with her mother, Dragon sits next to me on the couch. I still want to know who he is. And why does he act so strange? With nothing else to do, I decide to strike up a fake conversation with him. "So you like this party?"

He ignores me. He doesn't say anything to me. He just keeps his eyes in the direction of the party. *Maybe you didn't hear me*, I think. So I ask him louder, "So you like this party?"

He doesn't say anything to me again. It's becoming evident that he don't fuck with me. I decide to leave him alone. Maybe it's a good idea that we don't be friends. That way if he has to kill me, he can do it without a conscious. Which I don't think he'll have a problem with anyway.

I'm watching two little boys fight across the room, when a real pretty dark skinned girl approaches me. "You from Lavender Projects aren't you? I remember seeing you around before when I went to visit my cousin."

I look over at Dragon. He doesn't seem to be watching me.

"Yeah," I frown. "Why you want to know?"

"Because everybody here keeps talking about you. All anybody knew was that you were dead and now you're here. I tried to tell them that you not Crystal, but they don't believe me. They call you Twin right?"

I nod. " Yes. I guess I know why now. I apparently look like this Crystal girl."

She laughs. "Do you hang out with Champagne and Marcy all the time?"

"No. Today is my first day hanging out with Champagne. I never met Marcy before. Is she coming to this party? Because I heard so much about her, I feel like I know her already."

"Nobody knows Marcy," she says coldly. "Because just when you think you know her, she'll do something so fucked up that you'd think she's anything but the same person. Champagne can be a little different at times too, but that's only because she drinks a lot. They all drink a lot, especially Marcy though. Before Crystal got killed she drank a lot too." The girl laughs to herself. "Where I'm from, they call them the Drunk & Hot Girls. Because they pretty alcoholics."

When I look into the kitchen, I see Champagne staring at us. It doesn't matter that her mother is standing right in front of her talking her head off. Right now I'm the center of her attention.

"Do they know people call them that?" I ask the girl looking up at her. "Because I wouldn't like that name."

"I don't know if they know or not. But they do know they drink a lot. But, you don't get to drink that much alcohol, and not pay for it eventually with your looks. It just hasn't caught up to them yet I guess." She shrugs.

She's the first person to talk to me and not at me since I was picked up by Champagne. And, for some reason I feel like I can trust her. Maybe it's her angular nose, high cheekbones or big pretty eyes. But, I decide to ask more than I know I'm allowed.

"Should I be afraid?" I whisper so that Dragon doesn't hear me. "Of them? Well, of Champagne anyway since I haven't met the others. I mean do you think they killed Crystal?"

She looks at me, and then looks at Dragon and walks away without answering my questions. When I look at him he staring at me. I figure he heard my entire conversation. I can only imagine what he'll tell Champagne. She'll probably be really mad now.

Realizing I still hadn't gone to the bathroom, I stand up to find it, when suddenly my wrist is being squeezed by Dragon.

I look down at him. He doesn't say anything. He doesn't have to say anything. His eyes say it all. He taps the place under his shirt where he pulled the gun out earlier. In that moment he was saying that if I try to run again, he would waste no time killing me. And, I believe him.

When he finally releases me I go to the restroom, and knock on the door. Someone comes out and stares at me. He's a tall attractive older black man. He's wiping his hands with a piece of white paper towel.

"So you that girl they say look like Crystal?" He throws the paper in the trash by the door.

"I guess," I say under my breath.

"You look something like her, just prettier."

"Thank you."

"Well I'm going to tell you what the others won't. Stay as far away from them girls as possible. And that goes for my niece Champagne too. But, if I had to pick between the two of them, I would say be very weary of Marcy. The bitch is a killer. Now you look like a sweet girl, and I would sure hate to see you end up in one of them graves like the others. So you better get away from them while you still can." He places a hand on my shoulder. "Have a nice night. And, good luck."

# Day Two
# Thirsty Thursday
## Chapter Six

It's one o'clock in the morning and the car ride feels bumpier now than when I first got in. We're still riding in the Benz, but for some reason it seems like we're riding in something old. Like one of them buckets they be driving in the hood all the time that costs about three hundred bucks. It's probably my nerves.

I had already been scared of Champagne. But after talking to her uncle by the bathroom I was officially terrified. I had to admit if only to myself that Champagne is nothing like I thought she would be. She's still pretty. Still knows how to dress. But, she seems so sad. Like she's just moving around hour by hour just like me. Like she doesn't know what to do with her life, just like me. I always imagined she'd be stronger.

"Are you taking me home now?" I ask looking at her.

"I have a feeling you already know the answer to that," she says sarcastically. "So do you want me to tell you something you already know just to hear me talk?"

"I want to know when I will be going home," I say a little louder. "Not if I'll be going…but when."

She sighs. "When I don't need you anymore. Does that answer the question for you?"

I stare out of the window to my left. I look at all the cars passing by, and people going on with their lives. I wonder if they are happy. I wonder if they are in love. And, I wonder if they are like me, not knowing if they're going to see another day.

I lean back in my seat and close my eyes. My uncle comes to mind now. If I'm being honest, I'll say that I always knew what my uncle wanted from me. Sex. There were times when he would come over to my house, and watch me while I walked around. In a lustful way. I guess I never cared before, because at least he was there. At least he was giving me attention.

My daddy left me a long time ago. It was the saddest day of my life. They think I can't remember, because I was only three years old. But, I remember everything. I remember him fighting my mother with his fists. I remember her holding her eye with one hand, and the door with the other, demanding that he leave. I remember that kiss he planted on my lips right before he left. He smelled of alcohol...the strongest kind. I guess that's another reason why I don't like liquor to this day.

The next thing I knew me and my mother was on a plane to Paris. That was a long time ago, but to me it was like yesterday. He was a white man, but it makes me no difference. I still love him. I wonder where he is.

"Before this day I used to look up to you," I told Champagne. "You were somebody I wanted to be like."

She turns around and looks at me. There was a look on her face, a strange look of appreciation...I think. I guess nobody ever told her that before. But, it was true. She was my idol, and now I hate her.

No sooner than she smiled at me, suddenly she looked angry.

Frowning at me now she says, "I never signed up to be anybody's role model, or idol. I can only be responsible for myself. And, you need to be responsible for yourself too.

Instead of looking for people to take care of you. Or protect you. You got a pussy, Porsche. Start taking care of your own self, and be a woman. And, then you can be your own role model, and you won't need anybody else to do that for you."

"I don't want nobody to take care of me," I tell her. "Even at home I take care of myself. So you don't even know what you're talking about."

"How the fuck were you taking care of yourself, when you don't even have money to your name? I had to front you the money just to get your hair fixed. Remember that shit? So any bitch that can't take care of her own hair appointments is not taking care of herself. Don't get it twisted."

"I got a right to know if you're going to kill me or not," I change the subject back. "To tell you the truth I don't even care anymore."

"Well if that's true, that you don't care anymore, it shouldn't matter what I tell you. Now should it?" She presses the large red cup in her hand to her lips. I guess her crystal flask is empty now. From back here I can smell the candy and vodka smell from her cup. *Drunk bitch.*

"Can you at least tell me where we going now?" I ask.

"I have a question for you," she says. "Before I picked you up on the side of the road, with your underarms stinking, and your pussy ringing, what were you doing with yourself?"

I move uneasily in the seat. Champagne has a way of making me feel lower than her. I wonder if she's like this with everybody or just me. I also know where she's going with her question. She thinks I didn't have a life. And, that I was bored out of my mind. She was right. But at least it was *my* life, and at least I had control over it. With her I have control over nothing. I feel like a hostage.

Instead of giving her what I think she wants, I say, "What are you talking about?"

"Bitch, you know exactly what I'm talking about," she yells. "You weren't doing anything with yourself before I slid up on you. You had no life. I did you a favor. You had no existence. At least now whether you live or die, your life has a purpose. So I suggest you sit back there, keep your fucking mouth closed, and relax."

I should probably stay quiet. I probably shouldn't say anything else to her. But, I'm tired of being used by people. So I say, "You may have access to this beautiful car. You may even be prettier than me. And, you definitely have a better body than I do. But, let us not forget that you need me more than I need you. If that wasn't the case I wouldn't be here now. With a hairdo you paid for, and the only designer clothes I've ever worn in my life. Catch that."

Instead of getting mad at me she does something different. She says, "You got me right there. I do need you more than you need me. Which is why I'm going to keep you for as long as I have too. And, there ain't shit you can do about it. Now catch that."

We don't say anything else to each other. Instead we sit back and stare out of the window. From the corner of my eye I can see her look at me every so often. But for the most part she leaves me alone to sit in my own thoughts. I guess it makes sense, because what else do we have to say to each other that hasn't been said already?

Eventually we pull up to this beautiful brick house in Virginia, and I wonder who lives here. Dragon parks the car behind a pretty black Bentley. We all get out of the car and walk toward the door. Champagne knocks two times, and the door swings open.

Some woman who's kind of hard to describe opens the door. I could tell you that her natural silky black hair hangs down her back, and falls on the pink silk blouse she's wearing. I can also tell you that the blue jeans that hug the curves of her hips make her body look unreal. Like one of them video models. I could also tell you that her long eyelashes highlight her green eyes beautifully. But, my fear is that you still wouldn't understand how pretty she is. She runs rings around Champagne, and that's kind of hard considering they're both dope. I've never seen a woman this beautiful in person, in my life.

"Bitch, get your ass in here," the girl screams to Champagne. Dragon and me stand behind Champagne. "I knew you weren't going to let me down, and leave me in this shit by myself with Crystal."

"I'm mad you would even come at me like that. When have I ever left you anywhere?" Champagne frowns.

"I know, girl. But we've never been in no shit as deep as this before either. I think we fucked up this time. Don't you?"

My ears are perked. I feel like whoever this girl is, she's about to tell me what I'm doing here. She's going to tell me why I'm not allowed to go home. And, that if I stay quiet enough, Champagne will forget I'm behind her and let her continue to talk.

Instead Champagne turns around and looks at me. She turns back to the girl and says, "We'll get into all of that later." She pulls me closer to the girl by my hand. "This is the chick I was telling you about. The one who looks just like—"

"Crystal," the girl says finishing her sentence. "I mean I knew you said she resembled her, but they look like twins."

Champagne looks at me again. "I know, I know," she repeats.

"Well let me stop being rude," the girl says opening the door wider. "Come on in ya'll. I was just about to fix me a drink and fire up a blunt." She hugs Dragon, and we all walk inside of her house.

Everything in her house is as pretty as her face. Her burgundy furniture, her plush green carpet, and her thick brown drapes are all like that. Her house looked like it was pulled out of a magazine. I took a seat on her couch, and it was as soft as I imagined. I must've been real stressed, because suddenly I could no longer hold my eyes open. Sleep was pulling me, so I let go.

When I came to I heard heavy whispering. It's the pretty girl and Crystal. I keep my eyes closed hoping I could hear something useful, because they think I was sleep. And, would be free to talk.

I crack my eyes a little to see where they were within the house. When I do, I see them in the kitchen. They both are slurring when they talk so I figure they are already drunk. Maybe now I can finally escape, and get the fuck out of here. Champagne is wearing a yellow top, and yellow panties. No pants. She also has purple rollers in her hair, and is pressing a green beer bottle to her lips. The way she's dressed I can tell she comes here often.

"So she actually went along with this," the pretty girl says to Champagne. "I mean who would risk their life for this shit?"

"She doesn't have a choice," Champagne replies. "And I think she finally realizes it."

The pretty girl sighs. "I know how Crystal got involved in this shit, since Brillo is her boyfriend, but why are we involved? Why is Axe after us?"

"Because we were in that car when Crystal picked Brillo up. So as far as Axe his concerned we're all involved," Champagne says drinking her beer.

"Champagne, you know I'm not scared of nothing or nobody. We been through everything together…you know this."

"Marcy, just say what's on your mind."

"Okay. If Brillo is gone, we will have to leave town. Axe would never let us stay alive if his brother is dead. You know that."

"Calm down," Champagne says. "The only person who may get the business if that nigga is dead is Crystal. We don't have anything to worry about. I know that's my girl, but I'm being real. The thing is, they have to find Crystal first."

Since I'm currently playing Crystal in this shit, I know now they gonna put all of this on me. So I stand up from the couch and say, "I need ya'll to stop fucking around with me right now. Is Crystal dead or alive?" I approach the kitchen. "I don't want to hear anymore that I don't have a right to know. Is this girl alive or not?"

"Porsche, go sit down somewhere," Champagne says to me. "You getting all worked up for nothing."

"I need to know if that girl is alive right now," I scream. "Either tell me the truth or kill me. Because, I'm not staying around here anymore."

"Champagne, didn't you tell this girl that Crystal was alive?"

"Marcy, shut the fuck up," she yells.

Oh my God. I just realized what her name was. I'm standing in front of the girl everybody told me to fear. Marcy. I don't know what I thought she would look like, but it definitely wasn't like this. She looks more like a model, than a killer. And, I can't see a bad bone in her body. I know immediately that people are exaggerating about how dangerous she was, just to try to get me away from Champagne. I hate liars.

"Don't tell me to shut up," Marcy replies. She looks back at me. "Crystal is alive, Porsche. I promise you."

I look between them both because I don't believe her. And I let her know what's on my mind. "Everyone has lied to me. Why should I believe you?"

"Because I'm the one who is going to show you that Crystal's alive. That's why."

# Chapter Seven

Why do I care so much about a person I never met before? But, I have to know what happened to Crystal. It's like I'm in one of those scary movies. Where you're in bed, when all of a sudden you hear a noise downstairs. Everything inside tells you to call for help first. But, something inside of you, deep inside of you, wants so badly not to be afraid. Maybe that's where I stand now. I'm in my bed, I hear a noise downstairs, and I want to conquer my fears. The difference is I know I'm making a great mistake.

At least there's one good thing that came out of today, and that's Dragon has left the house. At least for right now anyway. I don't know where he went and I don't care.

We walk into Marcy's bedroom. The whole room is as beautiful as the rest of the house, but I'm not surprised anymore. She's a fly girl. Although the huge black bed that sits in the middle of the room, on the plush white carpet is an eye catcher, what I notice first are the many gin bottles lined up along her dresser, and the walls on the floor. How can anyone drink that much liquor, and still look as pretty as she does?

Champagne sits her empty beer bottle down on the dresser, and grabs one of the gin bottles. She removes a plastic cup from a pack that sits next to the liquor bottles. She pours herself a cup, and sits on Marcy's bed.

"I know you just didn't make yourself a drink, and not offer me one," Marcy says to her. "After all this time your ass is still selfish. The fucked up part is that it's all free. You don't have to be a hog."

"Don't act like that," Champagne says. "You know I was going to fix you something." Champagne walks to the dresser and makes another drink. "Sometimes you extra sensitive."

"You mean you were going to make me a drink, before or after you went to sit down on my bed?" Marcy asks.

"I ain't got time for all that," Champagne responds. "You want the drink or not?"

"Bitch, you know I want a fucking drink." Marcy looks at me. "You want something too? Unfortunately I only fucks with one thing…gin. But, in my opinion that's all you need."

"I don't drink," I whisper.

Marcy looks at Champagne and breaks out into laughter. "Who in this day and age don't drink? As young as you is why not?"

I shrug. "I don't like how it smells. To tell you the truth, to me it smells like it would taste bad. I'm good over here, but thanks anyway."

"Listen, girlie, if you rolling with us you drinking. I don't fuck with squares," Marcy says taking her drink from Champagne's hand. "Go make her a drink, Champagne."

"No really," I say louder. "I don't want it."

"And you heard what I said didn't you?" Marcy responds. "Anybody in my house is drinking. If you don't drink you gonna make me think you police. And I don't fuck with police."

I don't understand. Why are they so pressed to make somebody do something they don't want to do? The only thing I want is to find out if Crystal is alive or not, and go back home. The fact that they are beating around the bush makes me think she isn't alive.

"Just one taste, Porsche," Champagne tells me. "It ain't like you can get hooked or nothing. This shit is like oil. It'll just loosen you up so that you can enjoy life a little. For goodness sake, Porsche…live a little."

Champagne hands me the drink. I think its gin. It smells bad, and suddenly I want to throw up in my mouth. They didn't even bother to offer me anything to chase with it. It's not like I drink all the time. It's not like I drink anytime, but I already know they don't care. I want to keep the peace.

So I say, "Thank you." I look at the white stinky liquid in my cup. "Can I have some juice? To drink with it?" The real reason I wanted the juice, was because I was going to throw the drink in the trash, and fake like I was still sipping liquor.

Champagne laughs at me and says, "I'll go get you something."

"You really are a square bitch aren't you?" Marcy shakes her head at me. "You wouldn't believe how far out of your league you are right now. You fucking with some professionals."

I'm trying to think up a good way to ask what I want to know. Is Crystal alive or not? "You said you were going to show me that Crystal is alive," I say reminding her. "I really, want to see what you were going to show me." I move to fake like I'm about to drink but it's too strong.

"I'm going to get into all of that. But, first I want to know how you grew up in DC and not drink? I really never met anybody like you before. Is your mother a nun or something?"

Talking about my mother sometimes makes me sad. I guess because we don't have the type of relationship that I think we should. I never told anybody how I felt about my mother. And, I'm not sure if I want to talk about it now. "She's not a nun. She's an artist. I mean…she *was* an artist."

Champagne comes back into the room with my glass of juice. I take it from her and say, "Thank you."

"It's cool," Champagne says. "It's iced tea. It's the only thing I could find in the refrigerator."

Marcy sits on the floor and leans up against the wall. "How does somebody become and artist and then stop?" Marcy continues. "Because, once a singer always a singer, and once an artist always an artist. You can't change what's in your blood or heart."

"Bitch, why is you in here getting so deep?" Champagne asks Marcy. "You always like to know what's going on in a nigga's mind. Just sip your shit, and chill the fuck out. Ain't nobody trying to hear all that bullshit right now. You blowing my high."

Marcy frowns, and looks at Champagne. "It ain't about getting deep. It's about finding out who the fuck you brought in my house." When she's done with Champagne she refocuses on me. "Like I was saying how is that even possible that you don't drink?"

"It has a lot to do with my mother."

"So why she ain't an artist anymore?"

"My mother still paints, but it's not the same. She used to do a lot of painting when she was younger and living in Paris. I spent a lot of time there as a child."

"Hold up, you lived in Paris?" Marcy asks.

"Yeah, but it was a long time ago," I sip my tea. "My mother created a lot of murals, and from what my uncle told me she made a lot of money. I think one day she was in Paris on a ladder painting a mural, and she fell off. So she was unable to do what she loved anymore after that. So she started drinking a lot more, and taking meds for her pain."

"Damn, your mother was on some serious shit with her craft," Champagne says. "She wasn't out here faking it." She sits on the floor next to Marcy. "You gotta be good if you in Paris painting."

"If that's what you call it," I say uninterested in talking about my mother anymore. "If you ask me she's just another washed up drunk."

I don't know how she got to me so quickly, since she was sitting on the floor, but before I knew it Marcy is over top of my head like the ceiling fan. She gripped my new bob hairstyle in her hands and pointed in my face.

"Listen, bitch, my mother has been dead for five years. So you don't get to come in here, and talk about your mother like she didn't give you life. I don't play that type shit. Understand?"

"Yes," I say trying not to shake so hard, because my scalp hurts. She releases my hair, walks across the room, and sits on the floor next to Champagne. Champagne's uncle was right about that bitch. She is crazy.

"Now finish telling me about your mother," Marcy says.

I swallow. "What else do you want to know?"

"What's her name? We can start there."

"Lucy Hall," I respond before sipping my tea again. Damn this shit is good. I sit the gin down on the dresser, and surprisingly they don't pressure me into drinking it.

Marcy leans in and says, "Hold up you not talking about the lady that does the tattoos are you?" Her face brightens and she seems intrigued. "You talking about *the* Lucy Hall?"

"Yeah that's her," I say. "She doesn't do tattoos, just the designs. So you know my mother?"

"Do I know your mother?" She stands up, and turns around. She raises her shirt. I see a tattoo in the middle of her back. I remember my mother designing that tattoo last year. It's of a lady in a yacht. And the tagline says, *Out To Sea*. I know it's my mother's design also because of the two butterflies on the top right that are real tiny. It's like her signature, and I'm surprised they allow her to keep the butterflies in the designs.

Marcy sits back down on the floor. "Your mother is the best tattoo designer ever. And you should be proud of that shit too."

Now I feel dumb. That someone else has to tell me to respect my mother. I guess there is more to my mother's talent than I realize.

I take another sip of my drink. Suddenly I don't feel so serious anymore. It's like nothing matters. I'm smiling right now, and I don't even know why. When I try to take another sip of my drink, I realize it's all gone.

I raise my cup. "You got anymore of this shit?"

Champagne looks at Marcy, and smiles. She focuses back on me and says, "Of course I do. You can have as much as you can drink." She leaves the room with my cup.

When I look at Marcy's dresser, I notice she has a bunch of prescription pills sitting on top of it. My mother's dresser looks the same. Mainly she keeps Vicodin.

"You sick?" I ask Marcy.

"No. It's just that when you've seen as much as I have in life, it's kind of hard to get sleep. So I'm prescribed sleeping pills. If I'm having a really bad day I take two of them, and won't get up until two days later. Whenever I do that, when I wake up life seems easier to handle. It's like I've slept my problems away."

Champagne returns with my drink. With a grin on her face she says, "Here goes."

I drink the tea so fast, that I let out a big burp when I'm done. "This is so good. What's in it?"

"A little bit of everything," Champagne says.

"Well what's it called?" I ask drinking the rest of it. I wonder will I seem greedy if I ask for another glass.

"Long island iced tea," Champagne responds, before laughing with Marcy. "It's one of Crystal's favorites. That's why Marcy keeps it in the refrigerator and on chill. You want some more?"

I nod my head up and down. Before I know it I've had two more long island iced teas. Now I feel like I'm floating. Like my feet aren't on the ground even though I'm sitting on the floor. It doesn't take me long after that to realize they spiked my drink.

"That stuff has liquor in it…doesn't it?" I ask swaying from left to right. I sit the empty cup on the floor.

Their heavy laughter answers my question. I guess I should be mad, and maybe I am. I can't tell right now, because I suddenly feel sick to my stomach. Like everything I ate at IHOP wants out of my body. I guess Marcy must've seen the look on my face because she isn't laughing anymore.

"You better not throw up on my floor," Marcy says. "I will kill you in here."

I'm thinking I don't have much of a choice at this point. But, before I can ruin her rug, both of them rush me and lift me up by my under arms. They take me to the bathroom, and drop me on the floor. Marcy raises the toilet bowl seat and leans me over it.

"Throw up in there," Marcy says as if I don't know that already.

It sounds like a waterfall is coming out of my body. I never felt this sick in all of my life. Every time I stop throwing up for a second, I start throwing up again.

Marcy and Champagne sit on the edge of the tub and look at me. I wonder what they think of me now.

"Is she dead?" I ask wiping my mouth with the back of my hand. "The girl Crystal?"

"No she isn't," Marcy says.

"I thought you were going to show me that she was still alive," I say throwing up again into the toilet. "You guys made me drink alcohol and get sick. The least you can do is be real with me."

Marcy takes the phone from her pocket and shows me a picture of myself. I know I'm drunk, but I don't remember taking this picture before. And, how did she get it. "That's me?"

They both laugh. "No," Marcy says. "That's Crystal. I snapped a picture when she called me on video chat. If you look behind her you'll see the clock, and time on the wall. This was taken at a train station. About an hour before you both came over my house. So do you believe me now?"

# Day Three
# Freaky Friday
## Chapter Eight

The rest of the day I was drunk seemed to be a blur. I remember Marcy and Champagne coming in and out of the room to check on me. And, I remember me going back into the bathroom to throw up, only to see Champagne sitting on the toilet, with a cigarette in one hand and a beer in the other.

"Use the guest bathroom," she told me. I was so drunk that I didn't even know they had one in here.

Before long I hit the bed. And, was so sick I couldn't get out of it.

But on Friday around 11 o'clock in the morning, I was laying face down in the bed, in Marcy's guest bedroom. I felt somebody laying on my back, holding me down, and pushing in and out of my pussy.

The person is breathing heavily in my ear. His pants sound like a dog sniffing around for food. He has me pinned down so hard that I can barely move. The only things that I can move on my body are my fingers on my left hand. The pillow partially blocks my view, and I can't see his face.

The bouncing back, and forth that he's doing as he rapes me, causes my stomach to churn. So I throw up again, on the mattress, but he doesn't seem to care. He doesn't seem to notice. I can't scream because he's taken away the air out of my lungs due to his body weight. Who is he? And, why is he doing this to me?

When he lifts up to grab my hips, as he continues to rape me from behind, I can finally breathe. I want to yell, and cry for help but I'm scared. All I want is my mother and to go back home.

*Dear God, I know I haven't spoken to you in awhile. Well, we spoke the day my life was changed, when I got into Champagne's car. But, I need you to help me get out of this situation alive. I realize I don't want an adventure anymore. I want to be safe. I want to see my mother's face again. Please God. Help me.* I say to myself.

It seems like the rape never stops. When I feel him about to enter my butthole, I think I'm about to die. His grunts get louder and louder. I wonder if this is Dragon, but I don't want to see his face. I don't want to know its him. I don't want to know who it is. All I want him to do is hurry up and leave me alone.

When he lets out a louder moan, I know he reached an orgasm. Inside of me. Now from the mirror I can see a man's profile. His skin is dark brown, and his hair is knotty. Like it has never been combed before. Now I'm crying. I don't know if it's because he's so unattractive or if just seeing him places the fear inside of me.

When the door opens, and I see Marcy's surprised face I yell, "Help me! Please!"

Marcy runs up to the naked man, and snatches him off of my body. I roll over and bring the covers closely to my chin. As if doing this protects me. He already took what he came for.

I can now see his face. Something is wrong with him. Like he has Down Syndrome or something. It doesn't make me feel any better, but at least I know he's not in his right mind. But are any rapist sane?

"Beeper, why would you do that? Marcy asks as she places his black shirt on his body. "I told you not to do this anymore to my friends." She buckles his pants.

"I'm sorry," he responds. His words are slow and drawn out. "I wanted her to like it."

I'm mad. I know he has slow brain, but I want him to be accountable for what he just did to me. I feel like if he can hold a sentence, he can answer to his crime. Nothing about what I just went through was pleasurable. My pussy is throbbing, and my lower back aches from him pressing down so hard on my body. I feel a sudden need to defend myself, but I'm in a house of lunatics.

"I didn't like it," I say to him through tears. "What you just did was mean and wrong. You hurt me just now," I continue.

Beeper, now fully dressed, breaks out into this loud cry. He presses his hands over his ears and screams out into the house. "Beeper sorry! Beeper really sorry! Beeper never meant to hurt you, Crystal. Beeper only wanted to make you feel good. Like I did last time."

Suddenly I'm so grossed out. I can't believe Crystal would actually sleep with this man. What kind of women am I around? I need to get the fuck out of this house. And, I need to do it now, before something else happens.

"Don't be so mean to him, Porsche," Marcy says. "He didn't know what he was doing to you."

I frown. "I doubt that very seriously. It sounds like your freaky ass friend has been over here fucking him. And, it seems like he remembers it too. Now I don't have a problem with him doing whatever he wants to her, but he can't go around raping other people whenever he feels like it. I don't care if he's retarded or not! He needs some fucking help."

Marcy places both of her hands along the side of his face. "Beeper, go get into the car with aunt Champagne and uncle Dragon. They are out front. I'll be out soon."

"I don't want to go. I want to stay here and make love to Crystal again."

This is one horny mothafucka! This has got to be a dream. My life can't be this weird right now. It just can't!

"Beeper, that is not Crystal," she says pointing at me. "That is auntie Porsche."

*No I'm not his aunt either.* I think to myself.

"Now go out to the car. I'll be out in a second," she says kissing him in the mouth. "I promise."

When he leaves, she walks up to the bed and sits down next to me. "You know you didn't have to talk to him like that right? You can see something is wrong with him."

"Oh please forgive me for speaking up about being raped," I say sarcastically. "How is this my fault?"

"Because he has down syndrome. It's not like he meant to do it on purpose. Don't you give a fuck about anybody but yourself?"

"Are you serious?" I lean into her. "I just got my ass taken away from me, and you coming at me about being mean?" I put my feet up flat on the floor, and put on my underwear and jeans. "Please tell me how any of this is my fault."

"It's not about being your fault. It's just about understanding that if he was in his right state of mind, he would never have done that to you. My brother lives here in the house with me alone. And, most of my friends know to lock the door at night before they go to bed. You didn't so you ran into a situation."

"A *situation*? Did you just say I ran into a situation? That brother of yours raped me. Let's call it what it is and nothing else."

"You don't remember me telling you to lock the door?" She asks staring into my eyes. "It was right after you walked in on Champagne using the bathroom."

I'm embarrassed. "I don't remember anything," I say putting on my clothes. I realize I'm wearing the same clothes now.

"Then that's on you. Not me. Or Beeper. I specifically told you to lock the door, and you got so drunk that you didn't remember. Sounds to me like this is your fault not mine."

"You know what it doesn't even matter," I reach into my pocket to be sure my $20 bill is there. I figure it has to be a bus line around here somewhere. Once I catch the bus I can go to the train station, and then to my house. I don't care what I do, I just have to get as far away from them as possible. I stuff the money back in my pocket. I move for the bedroom door, and am about to twist the knob.

"Where do you think you're going?" She asks standing up behind me. "I thought we already had an understanding. You're with us until this thing clears up."

I take my hand off of the door and look at her. "See this is just it, I don't know what this *thing* you keep talking about is. All I know is since I've been with Champagne I have had a gun pointed at me, I have been kidnapped, threatened, lied to, poisoned and the latest raped. That's the only thing I understand right now. So you have to excuse me if I'm a little confused."

"I'm not your friend, Porsche," she says in a flat tone.

"I never said you were."

"Good, because you need to understand that the only way you are getting away from us is when we give you a pass."

"I don't understand. Crystal is alive so what do you need me for? I don't want to be involved in any of this shit. I want to go home."

"We need you because Crystal is hiding out right now."

"Is she hiding or did ya'll kill her? Because I'm starting a think that you, and your friend Champagne are mental."

"It's a good thing you have an understanding about who we are, but let me be clearer, nobody is more mental than me. Not Crystal, and definitely not Champagne. I'm the worst villain you can imagine times two."

As I look her over, it's kind of hard to believe she's capable of anything dangerous. But the tone in her voice lets me know that it's possible. If I knew how long they plan to keep me, and if I knew what they wanted me to do, I guess it wouldn't be so bad. But, nobody is saying anything to me. They just talk around me and about me, like I'm not in the room. The only thing I know for sure is that they won't let me go. Part of me wants to try to get away anyway to see what happens. After all what they gonna do kill me? People saw us together.

"What if I run? What are you going to do then?"

"Let me show you something," she says leaving the room.

I really want to go out of the front door, but something, maybe curiosity, demands that I follow her instead. We go into her room, and I can still smell the heavy scent of alcohol everywhere. I don't want anymore. My stomach turns just thinking about it.

She drops to her knees, and looks under the bed. She pulls out a large navy blue photo album. She places it on the bed, and sits down. She taps a place for me to sit next to her. I walk over to her and sit down. She drops the book into my lap. It's heavy, and weighs down on my thighs.

"What is this?" I looked down at it.

"Open it," she says.

I open the book. There are a bunch of newspaper ads inside. I wish I knew where she was going with all of this. This is all so confusing. She's so confusing. She wipes her long hair over her right shoulder. Although I don't know what the articles mean, the smile on her face tells me that she does. And that she gets a strange pleasure out of them too.

The headline of one of the articles reads, *Man dies in sleep. Reason unknown.* The second article reads, *Woman missing for one year. Her body never discovered.* The third article says, *A couple is murdered in a suburban home. Suspect never found.*

I understand now. As I flip page after page, I see similar articles. In the end of each article a person either dies for unknown reasons, or is missing and never found.

I close the book and look at her. "So you…"

"I think you're smart enough to know what I'm saying without using the word. You asked me back in the room what would happen if you tried to run. If you ever have that thought again I want you to remember this book. You can survive, or you can end up as a story in my book. The choice is yours."

"I think I'll stay…I mean…I think I'll hang out with you both a little bit longer."

"Great! Now we have to get out of here. Axe hasn't heard from us, which means he doesn't have his brother. I heard he may be on his way here, and if is true, we could all end up as a story in his book."

# Chapter Nine

We been driving a long time now. I can tell by the signs on the highway that we are on our way to Philadelphia. As usual I don't know why. Although I delete any plans out of my mind to run right now, it doesn't mean I won't run later.

Eventually we stop in front of a large home. There are three cars in the driveway, a silver Mercedes-Benz, a white Range Rover, and a red Rav Four. Dragon parks and pulls up behind the Range Rover, and looks at Champagne.

"I'll call you when I want you to pick us up," Champagne says to Dragon. "I love you. Okay?"

Dragon nods. I still don't know who the fuck he is. And why doesn't he talk?

Champagne gets out of the car, and so do Marcy and I. We dropped the freak better known as Beeper off on the way to Philadelphia earlier, and to tell you the truth I was happy about it. My body can still tell that he's been here. And I hate him and Marcy for it. I didn't feel like hanging around him all day. But, I know it doesn't matter, because nobody cares about my feelings or me.

When we get out of the car, Dragon pulls off and leaves us behind.

We all walk up to the door, and Champagne knocks on it lightly. When no one comes out she knocks harder. When no one answers still she looks at Marcy and says, "I know he not crazy enough to set us up. When we came all this way."

"I would be surprised if he did, you know the only thing he cares about is Crystal. Trust me, he's home."

Champagne grins. "I know that's why I told him she was with us." She turns around and looks at me. "Just so you know Porsche is no more tonight. As a matter of fact until everything blows over, we will not be referring to you as Porsche. From here on out we are going to refer to you as Crystal, so get use to it."

I don't say anything. I just bite my tongue and wait. To think that just the other day I was walking barefoot down the street minding my own business, and now I was being forced to deny who I am, and what I believe. My life is a mess. There is never a dull moment with these two.

When the door finally opened, a white man probably in his late 40s was on the other side. He's wearing blue jeans and a white T-shirt. He's attractive. Champagne hugs him first, and Marcy hugs him second. But, for some reason his stare seemed to be fixed on me. Marcy and Champagne move out of his way as he makes the trip toward me.

"Crystal, you seem to be more beautiful then you were the last time I saw you." He pulls me to his chest and my face rests there. I want to fight to get away, but it's too late. He already has me in his tight embrace. "What have you done to yourself? You look more beautiful than I remember."

I look at Marcy and Champagne for some help. But, like always they left me stranded.

"I don't know," I shrug. "I guess I just tried to stay stress-free. And, eat right."

"Well it's definitely working," he says grabbing me by my hand, and taking me into the house.

"Don't forget about us, White Daddy," Marcy says. "We miss you too. Even though we already know that Crystal is your favorite." They follow us into the house.

"She's right. Crystal ain't the only one who takes care of you when the time is right. I know you haven't forgotten about us already," Champagne says.

He releases my hand and walks over to them. "How could I ever forget about you two? I thought about you ever since the last time I saw your faces. What was it…about eight months ago?"

Marcy closes the door. "About that. But it's more like a year. We didn't stay away from you on purpose. Life just got in the way. Don't worry though. Tonight we're going to make up for lost time."

He walks over to a large bar. And I'm surprised that outside of it being huge, there doesn't seem to be much furniture here. He has just the basics, a couch, a table, a loveseat, and the dining room table with chairs.

He grabs a bottle of gin, and vodka from underneath the bar and places them on the top. And, then he rinses two glasses and places them on top of the bar too.

"You know it's the only thing I could think about since you called and told me you were coming over," he says to Marcy. He pulls them both two large cups of liquor straight up, no ice, or juice. He grabs them and walks them over to Marcy and Champagne.

"Of course before we play with you tonight," Champagne says taking her drink from his pale hand. "You're going to have to take care of us with a little bit of pocket money. I ran into some bills I have to pay. I know you got us, White Daddy. Don't you?"

"Anything for my girls," he responds handing Marcy her drink.

He walks into the kitchen, and grabs a picture of Brown liquid from the refrigerator. I know exactly what it is. He looks at me and says, "You still drink long island iced tea right?"

I look at Champagne and Marcy. I can't believe they gave me Crystal's favorite drink, and got me hooked. It's like they're trying to delete my identity, and replace it with hers. Part of me doesn't want to drink, and my stomach still feels sour from my last taste. But, after everything I've learned, and everything I've gone through, I feel like one more drink won't hurt.

"Yes that's my favorite drink," I say. "Thanks for remembering."

Marcy and Champagne smile at each other, and wink at me. I guess it makes them feel good that they got me to do something I couldn't stand. I know they're playing mental games, but I don't know how to stop them. They seem much more easy-going with me when I don't fight back so much. So I'm going to go with the flow for as long as I can, until I get my chance to escape.

He hands me my drink, and half of it goes down my throat before I can even change my mind.

"Well ladies," he says clapping his hands together. "Everything is ready downstairs."

"Not so fast," Marcy says. "My hands are itching which means I need my money." She wiggles her fingers, and holds out her hand. "We might as well get that out of the way now, so that we can enjoy ourselves for the rest of the night."

"You don't beat around the bush do you?" He says. And, then he looks at me. "Crystal is not going to fake again on me is she? Because, the last time we were together she refused me."

"And yet she's still your favorite," Marcy replies.

"Answer the question, Bitch," he says quickly. "Don't fuck around with me."

To be honest, before that point I didn't think he had an angry side. He was all smiles and hugs when I first got here. Now here he is calling Marcy what I wanted to from the moment I discovered what kind of person she was. Something warm rushes over me, and I can't help but grin. I can't wait to hear her reply.

"She'll play along," she responds looking at me with the same evil eye she gave me when she showed me the photo book in her room earlier today. "You have my promise."

He digs into his pocket, and counts out $3000. My eyes widen. Although, I don't know what they want from me tonight, if I have to compromise myself, it would be nice to get my share of the payout.

Marcy takes the money and gives Champagne half. *Where is my cut?* I think.

I plan to ask her for it later. I don't do it now because they walk over to him, and plant kisses all over his face and lips. He places his arms around their lower backs, and kisses them mostly on the necks. They walk toward another door, toward the back of the house, and for a second I hope that they have forgotten about me. When they disappear into the door, I'm even more hopeful.

I think this is it. This is the moment I've been waiting for. I finish my drink and sit the cup on the bar. I look at the door behind me. The front door. I can feel myself sweating. I'm nervous. I want out of here, but I'm unsure if I can make it. When I turn back around to look at the door they entered, Marcy is staring me in my face.

"Remember what I said earlier. Don't make me have to do something I don't want to. Because, I will." She holds out her hand to me, and wiggles her fingers. "Now come on. White Daddy is waiting for you downstairs. And, we are waiting for you too."

I take her hand. When I make it downstairs, I notice a wide-open space, no furniture anywhere. It looks like people wrestle inside of here. It's large, and black mats are on every inch of the floor. Champagne is already naked, with not a stitch of clothing on her body. I turn back to look at Marcy, and although she had on clothes when she came to get me upstairs, now even she is undressed.

I look at White Daddy, and he's staring dead into my eyes. "Undress," he tells me.

Immediately I wonder what I've gotten myself into now. I do as he says, and with nowhere else to go, stand close to Marcy and Champagne on the wall. We stand side by side against the wall. I feel like a doll. Stiff and motionless. Finally he removes his clothing, and walks down the line. First he stops in front of Champagne. And, then he stops in front of Marcy. *Please don't pick me*, I'm thinking. *Please don't pick me*.

When he stops in front of me my whole body shivers. He places his warm hand on my shoulder, and then raises my chin, and kisses me softly on the lips. He's a good kisser. I know what's happening now. And, there's nothing I can do to stop it. But, instead of pulling me on one of those black mats, he picks Marcy. I'm slightly relieved.

Marcy seems too eager to join him on the mat. His eyes remain on me, but he pushes Marcy to her knees. She grabs his dick, which is extra large, and goes to work. She spits on it first, before stuffing the entire thing into her throat. She's licking it up and down, and side to side like it's a vanilla ice cream cone. With his dick firmly in her hand, she raises it slightly and licks his balls. The sound of wet dick sucking fills the basement. He points at Champagne, and she walks over to him.

He points behind himself and she faces his back. When I see her drop to her knees, spread his pale ass cheeks, and run her tongue into the crack of his ass, I think I'm about to throw up. When I look at his dick now, there's so much spit on it that it looks like somebody threw egg whites all over it. The black mat under him is covered in white spit.

Suddenly he pushes Marcy away like an empty plate, and focuses back on me. He points to me and tells me to come over to him. But I don't move. I can't move. I don't want to be a part of any of the sick shit they doing over there.

When I disobey him, and stay against the wall Marcy says, "Remember the book under my bed."

I'm walking toward him now. Scared and confused. I drop to my knees, since that's where he told me to go. My knees keep sliding in Marcy's spit, and it's hard for me to be still.

He strokes himself hard, until he appears to be thicker than he was before. After doing it about 10 times he says, "Open your mouth."

I do, and immediately I'm wet with a yellow liquid in the face. Yellow stuff pours out of his dick and splashes into my mouth. When I realize its piss, I spit it out, back away from him and vomit in the corner.

Fuck these bitches. I'm out of here! I pick myself up off the floor, and run upstairs. I'm already out the front door when I realize that I left my clothes in the basement. Look at me now. I'm completely naked, and outside of the house with nowhere to go. Marcy finally comes out, wearing a blue velour robe. She has a red one for me in her hands.

I think she's about to kill me until she says, "Put this on."

She throws it a me. I cover my body with the red robe, and tie it tightly.

"Later we're going to see Crystal. If you still want to leave then we won't hold you back. But, I can't let you leave tonight, Porsche." She lifts the gun in her pocket just enough so that I can see it, and not the neighbors. "First we have to get back in the house and take care of business. He's our best client, and it's time to make money."

Since they know what they want from me, I decide it's time to get paid. "I agreed to be Crystal, but if you want me to go back into that house, and let some white man piss all over my face and body, I need my paper."

She laughs. "Don't worry. I'll get you later."

The last time someone said that I got a Happy Meal. "Then you better shoot me. Because, I don't give a fuck anymore." I hold out my hand, and wiggle my fingers like she does. "Now where is my money? And, I'm talking about $1000."

"You got me on that," she reaches into her pocket and gives me my cut. "But now you got to do everything we say. Because, if you don't, it's like you're stealing from me. And I kill people who steal from me. Do you understand?"

I rub my hands over my face and say, "You have officially rented me out for the rest of the day."

# Chapter Ten

I'm lying across the backseat, with my head in Marcy's lap. She's stroking my hair softly, and it feels so nice. It doesn't take a rocket scientist to know that at this point I must be drunk if I'm letting this bitch touch me. But, for some reason I like how it feels. It's relaxing. Besides, I'm one thousand dollars richer right now. After everything I went through, I finally have something to smile about.

I found out something I like about alcohol. When I'm drunk I don't have to think about what Marcy's brother did to me. And, I don't have to think about all of the freaky things we did to White Daddy at his house. I don't have to think about Nita pointing a gun at me, or my uncle touching me the wrong way. Suddenly all is right with the world. I know it will all change soon.

White Daddy is a nasty man who promised me the world a million times when we were done fucking him. Maybe it's because after two long island ice teas, I let him piss in my mouth, face and breasts. The funny thing is, the only thing he seemed to be interested in doing to me was urinating on me. But, he had sex with Marcy and Champagne for hours. And, at some point I thought it would never end.

As Dragon drives down the street I wonder what crazy things they have in store for me now. I don't believe that Crystal is alive. If she is why won't they use her to play the sick games instead of me? Why are they so dead set on me being involved, and not her?

When we pull up to a park somewhere in Philadelphia I wonder if this is a game. I don't see anybody here, and since it's almost dark, I wonder if Crystal is really coming or not. We all get out of the car except Dragon. Champagne hands him something and we walk off.

We walk toward a park bench and sit down. I think Marcy and Champagne are worried, but I don't know about what.

Since Champagne is sitting next to me, and wearing a watch, I keep glancing at it to see how long we've been waiting. Before long an hour has passed with no signs of Crystal. I knew she was dead.

"Where is she?" I ask sipping the long island iced tea from a cup I took from White Daddy’s house. "We've been waiting for like an hour now."

"She's coming," Marcy says in an irritated tone.

"She better come," Champagne says. "She owes us."

"If she's alive, why is she hiding?" I ask. "I mean, why can't she just be herself? Why am I forced to be her?"

Marcy looks at me and sighs. I'm getting on her nerves, but she's getting on mine too. "I'm going to tell you what we probably should've told you before."

I'm so excited to hear her response that my leg shakes. I place my hand on it and press down to get it to stop moving. "Okay. I’m listening."

"I don't know why she's hiding," Marcy says. "Outside of that time she did the video chat with me, she's been avoiding us. I don't know was going on with Brillo, or if he's even alive."

"If he's her boyfriend why would she want to hurt him?" I ask.

For some reason I remember how cute he was.

"You're not listening," Champagne says. "We finally putting you on to some real shit, and you not using your ears. Maybe you should scale back on the drinks a little," she continues snatching the cup out of my hand, and drinking it herself. "I see you can't handle your liquor."

Marcy snatches it back from Champagne and hands it to me. "She needs all the drink she can get to loosen up." Marcy looks at me. "We've been friends with Crystal all of our lives. Since we're only 25," she looks at Champagne, "people don't respect our relationship. They think we're too young to be so close. But, it's true. We know everything about each other. This is the first time that I can truly say I don't know what's going on with Crystal. She's hiding something from us, but I don't know what. In other words, we can't tell you what we don't know."

"The fucked up part about it is that she has us involved in this shit now," Champagne says. "Axe wants his brother and pretty soon he's going to start leaving bodies around DC if he doesn't find him. And, we needed you to be Crystal to Brillo's sister, because the last time anybody seen Crystal she was covered in blood. Lying in the middle of the street. And, since she and Brillo were last seen with us, Axe is holding us responsible. So we needed you until we could find her again, and bring her back home."

"What if she doesn't come home?"

They don't answer me.

I'm still thinking about what she said when suddenly a girl my height, and wearing a bob like me walks toward us. When I finally see her face, I can't believe how closely we look alike. I can tell I have the same effect on her, because she keeps staring at me.

"Where did you find this girl?" She asks them.

"From the block," Champagne responds. "We needed her since you refuse to talk to Axe, and tell him where Brillo is."

"I'm sorry guys, but I really can't see Axe right now. I know this is wrong, but I don't have a choice," she says. "Please don't be mad at me."

"Well how long do I have to be you?"

"I don't know," she shrugs. "I guess for as long as you want to survive."

# Day Three

# Freaky Friday

# Chapter Eleven

Although it is summertime, the park is as cool as a fall day. I'm staring into Crystal's face. The girl who has given me so much grief even though I don't know her. The weirdest thing is that she looks so much like me that I don't understand why we aren't related. I guess it doesn't matter. All that matters now is that she returns back home to DC so that she can live her own life. This shit is dangerous for me.

"Crystal, you have to understand what's going on," Marcy says to her. "Nita came to the hotel because she was told from somebody that Brillo was with you, and us," Marcy points to her chest.

"Well it's true," Crystal responds.

"Yeah, but Nita thinks we did something to him," Marcy continues. "And, with everybody saying that you was seen on Minnesota Avenue with blood on your chest, they assumed you were dead."

"Had it not been for Porsche, pretending to be you, and telling Nita about a fake car jacking, Porsche may have been killed," Champagne says wiping her fingers through the loose curls in her head.

"They still think you are involved," Marcy continues. "You gotta come back with us and answer to this shit."

"And, I told ya'll a million times that I can't do that right now," Crystal says with tears running down her face.

"Crystal, I don't understand what's going on," Marcy says throwing her hands up in the air. "It's like you're avoiding us which is fucked up since we're friends. Even if you not real with these niggas on the street, you should be real with us. The bitches that have your back through thick and thin."

Crystal walks over to the bench, and sits in the middle of Marcy and Champagne. Tears continue to crawl down her face and fall onto the pink tank top that she's wearing. Crystal grabs both of their hands, and looks back and forth between them.

"I've done something bad," Crystal cries. "Really bad. And, I know it's wrong that you doing this on your own, but I can't deal with Axe or Nita right now. I need some time to get things straight."

"We know that you did something bad," Marcy replies. "What we don't know is what it is. So just tell us what's going on. Let us help you."

Crystal brushes Marcy's long silky hair back and says, "I can't. I'm sorry."

I feel like I'm watching a movie. Like what's going on right now is not really happening. The only difference is I can't stop this movie and watch something else. I'm apart of this drama, even though I don't want to be. The biggest thing I want to know is, why no one has asked is Brillo alive or dead?

"I'm just going to come out and ask," Marcy says. "Crystal, is Brillo okay or not?"

Finally. I think.

"Because, this nigga Axe is back in town and he's threatening to hurt our families," Champagne adds. "Now I know you've gone through a lot, even though I don't know what it is. But, you can't expect us to take on this bullshit by ourselves."

"And, then you got the nerve not to be answering the phone when we call you," Marcy says to her. "This is wrong, Crystal. You way out of line for this. If Brillo is not back home like yesterday, heads are going to roll."

"He's not going to hurt your families," Crystal says.

"How the fuck do you know?" Champagne yells snatching her hand away from her. "You're fucking Axe's kid brother. You not fucking Axe. He could care less about us and you don't know him good enough to tell us anything different. "

"It's like the only person she cares about is herself," Marcy adds snatching her hand away from Crystal also.

"That's not true," Crystal says wiping the tears off of her face. "You know I care about both of you, but if things were that simple this would be over now. And, I would be home and we would be running the streets. "

"Is Brillo alive or not?" Marcy asks with a frown on her face. "It's time to stop fucking around with us. Did you kill the nigga or not? We need to know if we should get the fuck out of town."

There is a moment of silence. A lot of silence. My heart is banging in my chest as I wait for her answer.

As I think back on all the times both Marcy and Champagne threatened me, and pointed guns in my direction, I don't understand why they don't just grab her by the hair and pull her to the car to take her back to DC. Why are they so patient with her? What is it about her?

I'm wearing the same clothes I had on three days ago. And, I still have a thousand dollars in my pocket that I haven't had a chance to spend. I want to go home, take a bath, and let this be over with.

"I'll tell you everything you want to know about Brillo, "Crystal says. "And, I won't hold back anything."

"Why do I have a feeling like there is a but to this situation?" Champagne says.

Crystal stands up and removes a bloody piece of folded paper from her jean pocket. I wonder who the blood belongs to. She unfolds the piece of paper, and it makes a cracking sound because it's hard, and stiff. She hands the paper to Marcy.

Marcy takes the paper from her hand and asks, "First of all, whose blood is this?"

"I said I'll tell you everything you want to know," Crystal says. "But, not right now. The less you know the better."

Marcy stands up, and now she seems angry. She has the same look on her face as she did when she pulled a gun out of her robe when I left the house after White Daddy pissed in my face. Marcy looks down at the paper, and then at Crystal.

"Crystal, I'm getting real mad now," Marcy says. "Tell me what's going on, and stop fucking around with us. I've dealt with this shit way too long. Who the fuck is Dixon Terry and why should we care?"

"The name on that sheet of paper is very important," Crystal starts. "I need you to find that girl, and bring her to me. She is holding some information about Brillo that I must have."

"Bring her to you where?" Marcy asks. "We don't even know how to find you half the time."

"Bring her to me here."

Champagne stands up and takes the sheet of paper out of Marcy's hand. She examines it and says, "This chick lives in southeast D.C. She a real big girl right?"

"Yes," Crystal responds.

"So, you want us to drive all the way to DC, and back here just so you can talk to this girl?" Champagne pauses. "I mean can't we do the shit over the phone."

"I want her brought to me," Crystal says sternly. "The phone won't do."

"But, why?" Marcy asks. "Why is this necessary?"

"Because it's important to me," Crystal responds. "And, like I said, she has some information about Brillo that I need."

"But, when is what we want important?" Marcy questions. "It seems like the only thing on your mind is what you want. You went right past what we said about Axe threatening our families."

"I need you to bring me that girl," she says pointing at the paper in Champagne's hand. "And I need you to bring her to me soon. You do that, and everything will be cool."

"And if she doesn't come?" Marcy questions.

"Well then you make her come," Crystal says. "It ain't like you haven't done it before."

Crystal looks at Marcy and says, "Where is the money you told me you were bringing for me?"

Marcy digs into her pocket and hands her all of the money she has.

"That takes care of what I borrowed from you," Marcy replies. "So the debt is clean now."

Crystal counts the money, and nods. "Yeah this takes care of it," she tucks the money into her bra, and adjusts her shirt. "Now bring me the girl."

Champagne walks over to the bench, drops to the seat, and places her face into her hands. She seems as irritated as I am with Crystal.

"We're going to do this," Champagne tells her. "But, if you cross us it will be the worst thing you can do to yourself. Understand?"

"And if you don't bring me that girl, it will be the worst thing in the world for you too," Crystal responds.

# Chapter Twelve

We watch Crystal leave the park and disappear around some buildings. It was like she vanished into thin air. For some reason I have a feeling that it may be the last time we see her. When she's finally gone we walk towards the car.

Champagne and Marcy seem sad. And, their mood makes me sort of nervous. I don't want them taking things out on me since I look like her.

"Where we going now?" I ask tugging at the belt buckle on my jeans. I was trying to find something to do with my hands.

"Don't worry about all that," Marcy says to me.

I'm use to their negative attitude toward me now.

"I hope you know that we aren't going to see Crystal again," Marcy says to Champagne. "She's really going to leave us to deal with this shit with Axe on our own. Meeting her today has been a complete waste of our time."

"And, you're telling me that for…," Champagne responds.

"So, you can be prepared for it," Marcy responds rolling her eyes. "Because, if we don't find Brillo all the responsibility will be on us. You didn't talk to Axe when he was in Jamaica on the phone. But, I did. He kirked the fuck out on me. He wants his brother, and he could care less about this Dixon bitch or anybody else for that matter."

"Marcy, I know all that already. But, what Axe gonna do if we don't find Brillo is not helping us right now. Now she said she wants the girl. So, let's bring her the girl and hopefully put this shit behind us. That should be our only focus. She's holding all the cards right now." Champagne pauses. "But, if something happens to my family...,"

"Why would you even think like that?" Marcy questions. "Don't put that energy out there right now. What you need is a drink."

Although before meeting them I didn't like alcohol, now taking a drink is the only thing on my mind. So a smiles spreads across my face when the topic of alcohol comes up. I want a drink too.

After all this time that I've hung out with them I realized I still don't know what's going on. At least I know Crystal's alive. It makes me rest a little easier, because at first I thought they killed her. Now if we can find Brillo, and take him back home to his family, I'll be free to go about my business.

When we approach the car I notice that Dragon appears to be sleep in the driver's seat. He must have a gun on him or something, because who would be that comfortable taking a nap in Philly? At night? In a Benz?

"Yo, what is Dragon doing?" Marcy questions looking at Champagne. "He better be lucky nobody jacked his black ass for his ride. Don't he realize we in Philadelphia? The home of auto theft and robberies?"

"Well we've been out here all night waiting for Crystal's ass, so he was probably tired, and dozed off," Champagne replies. "He'll be fine. I'll drive now."

When we all walk up on the car I immediately have a bad vibe. Something is wrong. When Champagne pulls open the driver's side door, Dragon's body falls to the ground.

"What the fuck?" Marcy says.

"Is he okay?" I ask.

"Daddy," Champagne says shaking him. "Daddy, wake up. What are you doing?"

I'm stuck on stupid. I can't believe that the same man who has been giving me the blues is actually her father. Now it makes so much sense. His over-protectiveness. His driving us around the city, and being her personal chauffeur, is all because he is her father. The only thing that messes me up is that he looks so young. Maybe he fucked her mother when he was real young, because her mother looks old.

When I first met him, when they picked me up on the side of the road, I thought he was her boyfriend. Or some nigga she was fucking for paper. He's her father. Now I'm thinking about when we were at Champagne's goddaughter's party, when Champagne's mother said, "I can't believe you're still dealing with this no good ass nigga either." She was probably saying it, because they had a relationship, and it didn't work out.

"Champagne, look at his arm," Marcy says pointing at it.

When I look down I notice a needle hanging out of his arm. I cover my mouth in shock. Does this mean he's not sleep? Is he…is he…dead? Before this point, I never saw a dead body.

Champagne screams the loudest I've ever heard anybody scream before. She drops to her knees, and pulls his upper body to her chest. Dragon's head hangs to the right in her arms, and her tears fall onto his face. This is the weakest I've ever seen Champagne. To be honest, before this point I didn't think she had a soft bone in her body. She seemed so heartless…like a dude.

"Champagne, we got to get out of here," Marcy says snatching the needle out of his arm. She looks around into the night. "Before, somebody sees us out here, and try to jack us." She throws it on the ground.

Champagne looks up at her, and wipes her tears off of her face. "Bitch, this is my mothafuckin' father. He ain't some bag of trash you can just throw away. Have a little compassion for somebody other than yourself…damn!"

"He's dead, Champagne," Marcy replies stomping her high heel into the filthy ground. "There ain't nothing we can do for him now." She looks around again. "Now you know we got papers on us. You trying to get us locked up? Because, if we stay out here that's exactly what's going to happen."

Oh my God! They're wanted by the police too? Who the fuck are these bitches?

"I can't leave him like this," Champagne cries rocking him in her arms like a baby. "This is wrong. He would've never done me like this."

Marcy looks at me and says, "Porsche, go start the car. We gotta get the fuck out of here, and we gotta do that now."

I frown. "I don't know how to start no car." I play with my dirty fingernails. "I don't know how to drive."

Her eyes widen. "What the fuck do you mean you don't know how to start a car?" Marcy questions me. "What bitch alive don't know how to drive? What happens if a nigga takes you somewhere and you need to kill him and use his car to get back home? You'd be short."

"I guess so," I say feeling stupid again.

She sighs. "Well make yourself useful," Marcy continues. "Help me drag his body toward that tree over there." She points at a large tree to our right.

"If you touch my father, I will kill you," Champagne says to her. "And I'll kill you too," she continues looking at me.

Marcy punches at the air a few times. "Fuck! If you want to stay out here all night," Marcy says, "then knock yourself out. But, me and Porsche are getting out of here while we still can. And, we taking this car."

As Marcy walks to the car Champagne yells, "Wait!" She wipes more tears from her face. "Let me say goodbye to him first." She kisses him on the forehead. "Daddy, I love you so much. Thanks for not judging me, and for allowing me to be who and what I am. Although I know we haven't had the best relationship since you were in jail for most of my life, when we did meet up you made me feel so special. I just wish we had more time to spend together."

"We gotta go, Champagne," Marcy says jumping at every car that passes by. "And, we gotta do it now."

"I hate you so much right now," Champagne says to Marcy. "And I will never forgive you for this shit."

"Well at least you won't be in jail while you not forgiving me," she replies.

When Champagne is done saying her goodbyes, we drag his body to the tree, and lean him against it. Champagne kisses him one last time, and we rush to the car. Marcy moves to the front seat but Champagne says, "Get in the back. You not sitting next to me."

"Fine with me," Marcy responds with an attitude.

I slide into the front seat. Now that I'm up here, I can see all of the little bits of paper on the floor I saw the first day. I pick one of them up, and read it. It reads, 'Park the car and come inside'.

"What are these for?" I ask holding the sheet of paper in my hand.

Champagne wipes the tears from her face and says, "He couldn't talk," she continues down the road. "He was born mute."

I remember trying to talk to him at the party when we were on the couch. Although, I understand now that he couldn't speak, I remember a few times when he acted like he couldn't hear me too.

"I mean…could he hear?"

She continues to drive down the road. "Before he went to prison he could hear. But, he got into a fight with someone in prison. It was over a gambling debt. I guess he couldn't pay him. Anyway, the man promised to make him deaf too since he couldn't talk anyway.

"So when he was sleep one night he dug into his eardrums, and punctured both of them. That was that. He ain't heard good since. Sometimes he could hear sounds, but they have to be really loud. Like the popped balloon. Most times he read lips, but he has to be looking at your mouth. I never told anybody because he didn't want me too. Said he didn't want to be perceived as weak."

"I'm sorry to hear that," I say to her. I really am. No I didn't like Dragon, but now I think it's because I really didn't take the time to know him.

"Are you going to tell this girl the truth," Marcy says from the back seat. "Or are you going to continue to act like Dragon was the best daddy in the whole-wide-world?" Marcy pauses. "I'm just saying if you gonna cut out most of the story, don't leave out the important parts. Tell her how he's addicted to heroin, and how you supplied him everyday with a little baggie. I guess that last pack you gave him must've been foul," she giggles.

I think about all the times Champagne handed Dragon something, and how she would get mad at me if I approached her when she was doing it. Now I understand why.

"My daddy was a good man," Champagne responds.

"No, Sweetie, please do not sit up there and act like he was an angel. We both know it ain't true."

Champagne adjusts the rearview mirror. "You better be careful about how you come at me about my daddy. Because, whether you liked him or not, he was still my father."

"So I guess that means you aren't going to tell her the truth then," Marcy responds. "I guess I have to." I turn around and Marcy looks at me. "Her father was arrested for cutting off his ex-girlfriend's head when she told him she was pregnant. Because, he didn't feel like paying child support for yet another child. He wouldn't be home from jail now if there wasn't a technicality on his case. Some young law student in college found the flaw, and got him off. So don't let Champagne's tears fool you, because they don't fool me." Marcy laughs. "That nigga back there was far from a sweetie pie."

"One day me and you gonna have a problem," Champagne says to her.

"We got a problem now," Marcy laughs. "Now take me to Three Girls Swingers club. I'm broke and gotta make some extra cash."

# Chapter Thirteen

I've never seen anything like this in my entire life. At Three Girls Swinger Club, people were out in the open, having sex. In public. At first I was going to turn back around and run, but I don't know exactly where I am. All I know is that I'm in Philadelphia somewhere.

After Champagne paid for our admission, we walked into a larger room where it's dark. The only light on the dance floor is blue. The music is loud, and I can smell the scent of sex in the air.

I'm kind of scared about what's going to happen next. They already had me fucking some white man I didn't know, what were they going to have me do now? Fuck everybody in here for a few bucks?

I tap Champagne on the shoulder and say, "Can you get me a drink?" When a man touches my hand, I pull away from him, and move closer to her. My breasts rub against her arm. "I need something to clear my mind."

Champagne smiles and says, "I got you, but you need to relax," she smiles at me. "What you want, the usual?"

I nod.

She looks at my pocket and holds out her hand. I give her twenty bucks. She walks over to the bar, and leaves me alone with Marcy. They hadn't said a word to each other since we left the park. It doesn't seem like they plan on talking anytime soon, so I guess this will go on for as long as we are together.

"Relax, Crystal," Marcy says calling me by her friend's name. "Nobody in here is going to bite you, unless you want them to."

She smooth's her hair over her shoulder. She's wearing a cute little red dress and black shoes. Champagne is wearing a green one. They both look beautiful, and I look the same.

When I look down at her hand, I see she already has a brown drink. I guess she's feeling nice. "What kind of place is this?" I look around, hoping nobody touches me again.

"They call it a swingers club," she sips her brown liquor, and pulls her hair behind her ear. "I call it the bank of Philadelphia. Where I'm free to withdraw funds as I please."

I remember what Champagne said to me the first day I got into the car. She told me to always keep my bank clean. So I'm sure her calling this club a bank means it was another way for them to get paid, using their pussies of course. I hope this time they leave me out of it.

"Why you call it that?" I ask, standing so close to her that it seems like we're lovers.

"Because, these old ass couples in here will pay bitches like us to spice up their love lives. To make them stay married longer, so they don't have to cheat and leave the relationship."

"But, ain't they cheating by having sex with ya'll?"

"No," Marcy says dancing to a Lil Wayne song. "It's a mutual agreement so it's not cheating. Whenever we in Philly, me and Champagne hit this spot up. Trust me, you're about to make some bank."

"I'm not trying to fuck nobody else," I frown.

"Then you a, stupid bitch," she laughs in my face. "How long do you think that little cash in your pocket will last once you get home?" She pauses. "Days? Maybe," she shrugs. "The thing is you got an alcohol habit now. So you gotta feed it like it's a newborn baby. Not only that, you were probably fucking for free. Now the least you could do is get paid for it."

I feel like I'm drowning. "Is this why ya'll got me drunk? So I would need money, and sell my pussy?"

"We didn't make you do nothing," Marcy replies. "You took the first and last sip on your own. You need this gig, girl," she playfully shoves my arm. "So lighten up."

When Champagne returns with my Long Island Ice Tea, I drink all of it. I know I'm not old enough to buy another one, so I say, "Can you get me an extra drink please?"

"No," Champagne snaps. "It's time to get some paper, and have one of these freak niggas buy you one. Trust me, if you act right you won't have to use another dime of your own cash."

We walk over to the wall, and stand against it. A brown table thing runs horizontally along the wall. Champagne and Marcy turn down the first five couples who want our attention. But, when a black couple, about forty something approaches us, they both nod at each other and smile. I guess Champagne and Marcy aren't mad at each other anymore.

"Are you ladies voyeurs?" The woman asks us.

I look at the blue mini dress that she's wearing. She has a very pretty face, and light skin. Her brown weave is long, and her eyes seem innocent. I wonder what made her agree to this type of lifestyle.

"What's a voyeur?" I ask.

Champagne and Marcy immediately look at me with evil eyes.

"What I do?" I ask.

The lady laughs at me. "How cute," she scrubs my messy brown bob with her long black nails. "You're a newcomer."

I nod. "I guess so."

"Well voyeurism is when people like you come into the club and watch," the man says. The blue light bounces off of his baldhead, and makes him look alien. He's nowhere near as attractive as she is. "You girls don't participate."

"Who says we don't participate?" Marcy asks him.

"Well are you watchers or into fun and games?" He questions.

"We are into fun and games," Marcy responds. "Just as long as you both are generous."

The woman's eyes brighten. "We don't mind playing fair, if you ladies play fair."

"We are the best," Champagne responds. "But, we're off-premise type of girls. So I hope you all have somewhere for us to play privately."

"Sure we do," he says. "Follow us."

I'm sitting on the floor in the living room. My back is against the wall. Champagne is standing in front of me. We both are watching Marcy, Joey and her husband Peter on the sofa fucking hard.

Joey is sitting on the grey sofa. She's naked from the waist down. Marcy is on her knees, in between Joey's legs licking her pussy clean. Peter is behind Marcy, fucking her in her asshole. I guess there ain't nothing that Marcy and Champagne won't do for money.

While they are fucking this strange couple, I'm wondering when are we going to look for the person whose name is on the paper Crystal gave them, which is soaked with blood. It's like they don't care right now. Maybe they have a plan of their own, and aren't giving me the details.

"Damn your asshole is juicy," Peter says to Marcy. "And tight too. Just the way I like it."

His foot accidently knocks over the glass cup Marcy was drinking her gin out of earlier. It doesn't stop him from fucking her.

Marcy seems to be enjoying licking the flesh of Joey's pussy. Marcy is handling them both. She's winding her hips against Peter's dick, and causing him to moan out loud.

After five more minutes Peter turns around, looks at Champagne and says, "I'm ready. The marital aids are in the box."

Champagne wobbles on the way over to him. I can tell now that she is drunk. Extra drunk. She can barely stand up straight. This is the first time I saw her this drunk. Before, this it seemed like she could handle her liquor. I guess she's still thinking about her father, and the way he died. That's all she talked about on the way over here. All the things he did for her. It's kinda sad.

Champagne goes to the box by the couch and opens it. She grabs the black strap connected to a rubber brown dick. She slides out of her jeans, and panties, and they fall to the floor. She attaches the strap to her body, and strokes the plastic dick twice, before she drops to her knees. She spreads his meaty brown ass cheeks, and slides into him.

My jaw drops. I'm currently watching Joey on the couch getting her pussy ate out by Marcy, while Peter is fucking Marcy from behind, while Champagne is fucking him. I'm mad at myself because somewhere inside of me, I'm turned on. They sound like they're having such a good time. I want to participate but I wouldn't know what to do. Maybe the liquor I've been drinking all day got me buzzing.

When Marcy gets up, she taps Joey on the shoulder. Joey lies on the couch the long way. Marcy sits on Joey's face, and at first I think that she's going to smother her. But, Joey grabs Marcy's waist and seems to be pulling her closer to her face. Marcy is grinding her ass on Joey's face like she's trying to suffocate her.

They not the only ones getting it on. Peter is now lying on the floor while Champagne continues to fuck him from behind. This is the wildest thing I've ever seen in my life, and I'm so turned on right now that I ease out of my jeans, and panties. I open my legs and slide my fingers in and out of my wet pussy. My syrup slides out and onto the floor underneath my ass.

I'm about to cum when Marcy reaches on the side of the couch and pulls out her gun. She rises off of Joey's head and shoots her in the mouth. When Peter tries to get up, while Champagne is still fucking him from behind, Marcy fires into his chest first, and then his chin. He drops on the floor, and Champagne slides out of him.

I scream loudly until Marcy points the gun at me. "Shut the fuck up," she says looking at my naked bottom. "And, put your clothes back on. You having too much fun. This is work."

I'm embarrassed and scared. "Why…why did you do this?" I look at their corpses laying over the living room. "They were nice people."

"They were freaks," Marcy responds placing her clothes back on. "Now hurry up and get dressed and let's find some money around here."

Champagne removes the strap-on and jumps back into her clothes. They both disappear into the house.

I know what Marcy wants me to do, but I can't move. I'm sitting on the floor, legs spread eagle, looking at dead bodies. Dragon was the first dead body I saw before. I hadn't planned on seeing another one in this lifetime. I guess I was wrong. I put my clothes on, and stood by the front door.

I'm shaking.

I'm shaking.

I can't stop shaking.

After destroying the house, I see them come back into the living room with a bunch of money and jewelry in their hands.

"Let's get the fuck out of here," Marcy says.

We are about to walk out of the house when a little girl with long black pigtails comes out of the back. She looks about ten years old.

"Mommy…daddy," she says in a low voice. When she sees her parents bloodied bodies she cries loudly. "Mommy!"

"Fuck," Champagne yells. "A kid is in here. Them freaky mothafuckas left a kid by they self in the house!"

"We gotta kill her," Marcy says. "She seen our faces."

My heart drops into the pit of my stomach.

"We not killing no kids," Champagne responds. When Marcy cocks her gun Champagne says, "Did you hear what I just said? We not killing no fucking kids, Marcy. What is wrong with you?"

"I told you," she says. "She saw our face."

"We will be good, so lets just get the fuck out of here." Champagne looks at the kid and says, "Listen, do you see what we did to your parents?"

The girl is shaking too hard to respond.

"If you tell anybody we were here, we will hurt you," Champagne continues even though the girl doesn't answer. "Okay?" The little girl isn't responding and I'm scared for her. I'm scared for both of us.

"Let's go," Marcy says. "I'm not going to hurt her."

We all leave out of the door. We are in the car, and about to pull off when Marcy says, "Oh shit, I forgot my glass cup. I drank out of it earlier, and it has my fingerprints all over it."

"And your butt juice is on Joey's face," Champagne says. "You gonna cut that off too?"

"Don't start with me, Champagne," Marcy says. "Let me go into the house, and get the cup. I'll be right back."

I watch her go into the house. My leg is trembling, and I don't know how to make it stop. When I hear one gun shot, followed by another, I know what happened. The house door opens and Marcy runs back outside. She did it anyway. She killed the kid.

# DAY FOUR

# SEXY SATURDAY

# Chapter Fourteen

I see crazy colors right now while I'm laying horizontally in the backseat. Everything is blurry. I wonder if I'm flying. Real high…because all I see is blue skies. I don't have a problem in the world right now. Not one. Thanks to the drink in my plastic up.

"You alright back there?" Marcy asks me from the front seat.

She killed the little girl. How could she kill a little girl yesterday, but be so cool now? I wish I could be like her. Heartless and mean when I want to. But, I can't. I care about what happened to Joey and Peter. I care about what happened to their daughter, and I care about what happens to me.

"I'm fine," I say to her. Stretched out on the back seat is still my favorite place to be. "I could use another drink after this."

"We'll stop by the liquor store later," Champagne says.

Champagne is different now. Ever since Marcy killed the little girl, and made the comment about her father, she seems to be tolerating her. It's like she doesn't like her anymore, and if she says one last thing, she will go off on her.

"Let’s get some drinks now," Marcy says to Champagne. "I haven’t had nothing all day either. I need a buzz. And, as uptight as you are, you need something too."

"Marcy, don’t tell me what the fuck I need," Champagne responds to her. "You need to focus on yourself, instead of worrying about me and my business all the time." She laughs to herself. "On second thought, let me scratch that. You give a fuck about yourself too much as is."

Marcy laughs and sits back into her seat. "So let me get this straight, you still mad about what I said about your father?"

Champagne looks at her and frowns. "What you said about my father? Bitch, I’m mad that you killed a little girl for no reason. How come whenever you move, you gotta leave bodies in your wake? I mean, I was with the weirdoes dying, but killing the girl was wrong."

"She was a witness," Marcy laughs. "Not a little girl. And you should be thanking me. I’m the only one between the three of us who doesn’t have a problem with busting my gun. You need people like me in your camp. So give me my props, and chill the fuck out."

"Marcy, you need help," Champagne says shaking her head. "A lot of help. That’s why they took your daughter from you, because you weren’t responsible enough to watch her. But, at least with the Chinese family she has a chance at a real life. And, safety."

Marcy took her entire hand and smashed the side of Champagne’s face. Her head bangs against the window. The Benz whips to the left, but Champagne gets the car quickly back under control. She parks the car, jumps out and moves to Marcy’s side of the car. She pulls on the door five times, but it doesn’t open.

"Open this door, bitch," Champagne taunts Marcy while cracking her knuckles. "You put your hands in my face, so come on out and fight me straight up."

Marcy shakes her head and laughs.

"I'm not playing," Champagne continues. "Why don't you come out here right now and do that shit again."

I can't believe things are going this far. I sit up and look at Champagne circling outside of the window like a shark. Champagne's so mad that her entire face reddens. I don't know what's about to happen, but I hope nobody else gets killed.

"I'm not going to fight you, Champagne," Marcy responds looking unfazed. "So just get back in the car so we can find this bitch that Crystal wants. We wasted too much time already." She pauses. "I'm not playing with you. It's time to go."

"If you scared to fight me, just say so," Champagne says. I can tell she wants to battle badly, because her nostrils are flaring.

Champagne takes five more minutes to stare Marcy down. I'm getting bored with this now. I'm hoping Marcy gets out, and fights so we can move on. But, Marcy doesn't leave the car. Instead she remains seated.

Eventually Champagne gets back into the car. "If you ever put your hands on me again, Marcy, we won't be friends anymore," she says pointing in her face.

"And, if you ever say anything about my daughter again, when you know how much she means to me, I'll kill you with my bare hands," Marcy responds looking at her.

"I guess it is what it is," Champagne replies.

When we make it to the high school, the pit of my stomach rumbles. Not because I'm scared, but because I hate school. All schools. I feel like somebody is going to make me go to class, and do some work. I want to hurry up, and get out of here.

Marcy, and I stand next to the girl's bathroom. We're waiting on Champagne to come back. It feels like forever, but she finally returns. "She'll be here in a minute. I paid some stupid ass kid to tell her to meet me in the bathroom."

"Who did he say that you were?" Marcy questions.

"Somebody who is unloading some Vicodin," she responds. "I asked around about her before I did anything. I found out she's a pill head. When I told the kid I had some, the rest was easy."

We all walk into the bathroom. The smell of Pine Sol and dirty toilets makes me sick. I gotta get out of here.

About five minutes later a fat girl with a wild curly weave and big eyeglasses comes into the bathroom. She stands next to the sink. At first she looks stuck and I wonder why.

"Which one of ya'll got the pills?" she asks us.

"I do," Champagne replies walking up to her. "You got my money?" She holds her hand out.

The girl goes through her purse quickly. I guess she can't find the money right away, because she starts throwing things on the floor. She seems nervous. Really nervous. First some keys fell onto the floor, and then her makeup.

When she is done dumping everything out of her purse, she finally finds the cash. "Here it is," she holds the dirty green twenty dollar bill in her hand. "Mike said it was twenty right?"

"Yeah, that's about right," Marcy says walking up to her, and taking the money. "But, before we get into all of that we got to ask you a couple of questions. First off, what's your name?"

"A couple of questions," she says softly. "I thought this was about the pills."

"It is," Champagne says. "It's about the pills and so much more."

"Okay," she says in a low voice. "My name is Dixon. Dixon Terry."

Marcy and Champagne smile at each other. The way they always do when they know something everybody else doesn't.

"What else do you want to know?" Dixon asks them.

"Do you have a boyfriend?" Champagne questions.

"Uh...yeah...why you ask?"

"What's his name?" Marcy responds. She's so close to her now, that if the girl backs up, she'll bump into Marcy's titties.

"Ya'll don't know...h-him," Dixon stutters dropping to her knees to stuff the things back into her burgundy purse. "He don't go to this school. He older than me anyway."

"I didn't ask you if he went to this school, bitch," Marcy yells. "I asked you what is his name."

"Look, I don't know who ya'll are, but I gotta get back to class," she stands up. "Excuse me."

When she moves to walk around Champagne, Champagne pushes her so hard into the sink that she made it hang a little lower. Then she walks up to her, and gets into her face.

Marcy takes the black glasses off of Dixon's eyes, and drops them to the floor. And then she steps on them, and smashes the lenses.

"Oh my God," Dixon screams. "You just broke my glasses."

Marcy squeezes her throat and whispers, "You better lower your fucking voice. Trust me, you don't want to fuck with a bitch like me."

"Now we not gonna keep asking you," Champagne says in a low voice. "If you say you got a boyfriend, all we want to know is his name. So what is it?"

"I...I...um...he...," she couldn't seem to get his name out.

As they corner her, I realize I don't know the purpose of all of this. How does this girl relate to Crystal? After four days of being with them I now know that what I think doesn't matter. I don't question them about much anymore. I just go with the flow. Besides, I'm starting to like their company. Being with them makes me feel like a rebel sometimes. Like I'm running from the law. Maybe I am.

"Bitch, how come you don't just tell us what his name is?" Marcy questions, yanking her hair.

"His name is Brillo," she whispers.

Champagne looks at Marcy. They both seem angry.

Now I understand why Crystal wanted us to find her. Maybe she wanted to get at this girl because Brillo cheated on her. But, when I look over the girl's body, I don't believe he would want someone like her. Crystal is pretty, and this girl is ugly. It doesn't make any sense.

"If he is your boyfriend, where is he now?" Marcy asks.

"He's at my house," Dixon says softly. "Well he will be coming over my house later."

My eyes widen. I just knew Brillo was dead. If he's really coming over her house, we can let his family know and bring him back to them.

"Are you fucking around with us?" Champagne yells. "Because, we don't like games."

"I swear on everything," the girl cries. "He's my boyfriend, and he's coming over my house later."

The next thing they do is crazy. They beat her so badly that her blood is over everything in the bathroom. When they are done, they pick her up to her feet. She can barely stand up on her own.

"That's for our friend," Champagne says. "Since you want to fuck other bitch's niggas."

"Now you gonna take us to your house," Marcy adds. "And if Brillo doesn't come over, you're done."

# Chapter Fifteen

Dixon's house is old, but cozy. The newest thing in the house from what I can see anyway is the flat screen TV on the wall. What bugs me the most is the smell in here. The awful sweet stank that seems to be in every area of the living room. I try to ignore it, because I seem to be the only person bothered by it.

I'm sitting in an old green loveseat, across from the sofa where Marcy is sitting. Dixon is sitting on a large black plastic pillow on the floor. Champagne is standing up in the kitchen.

When I look down at the coffee table, I see a lot of books about theater and acting. I figure Dixon is taking it up in school or something. If we had classes like that in my school, maybe I would've liked it more.

We been in Dixon's apartment for an hour waiting on Brillo. To be honest I can't wait to see his face. I feel like I know him already. Since we shutting the city down to save him, it would be nice to meet him personally though.

Although I'm excited about seeing this legendary Brillo, Champagne seems really sad. She keeps saying that she misses home, and wants to go home and check on her mother and family. Marcy talked her out of it five times already, because we didn't know where Axe was in the city. Marcy said it was best to stay away from her mother, because with Axe back in town now, he's liable to spot her.

Champagne is on her cell phone now, dialing another number. Like she did the first fifteen times, she hangs up with another attitude. "Nobody at my house is answering the phone," she tells Marcy. She plops on the sofa next to her.

"Maybe your mother is mad at you," Marcy says sitting closer to her.

"When I was at my God daughter's party I gave my mother fifteen hundred dollars for rent for two months. The last thing my mother will be is mad at me," Champagne responds. "I just hope they are okay."

"They are," Marcy says slapping her on the back. I heard the sound all the way over here so I know it had to hurt. "What I want to know is why Crystal is not answering the phone again? We couldn't deliver this bitch today if we tried."

"Something is up with her," Champagne says pointing at Marcy.

"You think?" Marcy responds sarcastically.

"I'm so fucking stressed," Champagne replies.

"You'll be fine," Marcy promises. "Everything will work out. Now drink this," she bends down and hands her the cup of gin she's been nursing since we first got here. "Sip on this."

"You know I don't want that shit," Champagne says pushing it away. "I need something else." She looks at Dixon. "Your folks don't have no vodka in here? Or anything else but gin?"

"My father also drinks beers," Dixon says in a soft voice.

"Go get me one then," she orders.

Dixon rolls off of the pillow. Once on her knees she uses the floor to stand up straight. Before making it to the kitchen she bumps into the couch, and the kitchen counter. I guess since Marcy smashed her glasses she can't see straight.

When she's finally in the kitchen, she grabs something brown in a bottle from the refrigerator, and brings it back to Champagne.

Champagne takes it out of her hand and frowns, "This is root beer," she yells. "I said bring me a beer." She shoves it toward her.

"I'm sorry," Dixon says taking the drink back. "I can't see so it's hard to choose the right thing." She walks back into the kitchen, bumping into everything in her path. She looks like one of them balls in a pinball machine right now. She eventually makes it to the refrigerator, feels everything inside and returns with a green bottle. "Is this what you want?"

Champagne snatches it out of her hand, "Yeah…this is good."

Dixon drops to the floor, and crawls on her knees to the pillow again.

"What's that you sitting in?" Marcy asks Dixon.

"A floor pillow," she says softly. "It was for my dog."

"What happened to him?" She asks.

"He ain't make it," she responds in a regular tone. Like nothing is out of the ordinary.

"Well why he ain't make it?" Marcy says.

"Because, I didn't like him," she says. "He use to bite me too much. They called it play nibbling, but he was ninety pounds, and the shit hurt. So he had to go."

Marcy and Champagne look at each other again and laugh. I hate them sometimes. It's like the entire world is here for their amusement. They can be so selfish and sneaky.

Out of the blue Dixon starts crying. Really loudly. Like she just found out her dog died at that moment.

"What the fuck is up with you?" Champagne asks her. "Why you crying all of a sudden?"

"What do ya'll want with me?" Dixon questions. "Why are ya'll in my house? I don't even know ya'll."

"Because, we have a mutual friend that's why," Champagne tells her. "And, there ain't no need in you crying about it. We not leaving here until Brillo comes through that door."

"But, what did I do? Why are ya'll so mean to me?" she wipes the tears off of her face and looks at them. "All I did was love Brillo."

"Well the nigga you loved belonged to somebody else," Marcy says in an evil tone. "Now people had to make up stories, because for whatever reason, he not going home. And, since he's not going home, people are looking for us. So we got some questions to ask him. And, if ya'll want to be together after that, then that's on you."

While they are interrogating her I can't get over the smell in here. It's real strong, like if we stay any longer, it will seep through our skin and hair.

"I don't even know why Brillo would deal with a bottom feeder like you," Marcy says helping herself to some more of Dixon's father's gin. "You not his type. What you know how to do? Suck a good dick or something? I mean can those teeth come out of your mouth?"

"What you mean bottom feeder?" Dixon says, as her voice gets deeper. "Every girl doesn't have to look like you to get a man."

"Uh…yes they do," Marcy laughs. "If you want to get a man of a certain caliber, and keep him, you have to look just like me or better. And, you don't." She points at her. "Which is why I'm interested in this whole situation, and how ya'll got together."

"You know Crystal?" Champagne asks her.

Dixon looks at me. "I know the real Crystal," Dixon replies. "And, she never knew what to do with a man like Brillo. He needs somebody who can love him like he needs to be loved. She ain't good at it. She fights him too much, especially in public."

"If you know Crystal, then that means you know us too," Marcy says pointing at her.

"Yeah…I knew who ya'll were when ya'll came into the bathroom," she says repositioning her body on the pillow. "I didn't know this was about Brillo though." The girl suddenly frowns. "Wait, are ya'll fucking Brillo too?"

"Bitch, I'm asking the questions around here," Champagne yells at her. "If you knew who we were, why didn't you try to run? Or leave?"

"Because she was pointing a gun in my lower back," she says pointing at Marcy. "And I didn't want to die on no bathroom floor at school. So did I answer everything you wanted?"

I didn't even know Marcy had her gun out. She is scary.

"You not out of the clear just yet, hog," Marcy, tells her, helping herself to some more gin. "You better hope your boy comes through this door within the next hour."

"He will be here," Dixon replies. "He loves me. A lot too. And, there ain't nothing ya'll can do to change that."

"Did your dog die in here?" I blurt out pinching my nose. The smell is strong. Very strong.

"Yes," she responds. "He died earlier today, before I went to school. I didn't know he was dead, because I'd been poisoning his food for so long, and he never moved. I thought he was just sleep."

I hate this girl. Who kills a dog?

"Where are your parents?" Marcy says giving her another evil eye.

"Out of town," she says slowly. "Why? You want to threaten them with guns too?"

"You think you're cute don't you?" Marcy asks her. "If you do you need not think that anymore. You're anything but cute."

"Beauty is in the eye of the beholder," she says.

"Ain't nobody beholding your beauty," Marcy giggles. "Brillo may have beheld your pussy, but it was never your beauty. Trust me, I know the kind of nigga he is. And, you are in anything but his league."

"Then I guess you don't know nothing about nobody then," she laughs. "Plenty of big bitches snatch dudes from chicks like you everyday. It's becoming common."

I can't take the smell anymore. I stand up, and sniff where I am. I go behind the couch, and over to the kitchen. I sniff harder but the scent is not as strong.

"What are you doing?" Marcy asks me. "Sit down, you acting weird."

I ignore her. I sniff in the kitchen, by the trash and even inside of the refrigerator. I walk down the hall and sniff there too. The smell is strong now. So strong my eyes water. When I sniff past one door it isn't as strong. I move to the other, the one toward the back of the apartment. I sniff again, and the horrible scent rolls through my body.

I put my hand on the knob, and turn it slowly. The door opens. When I push the door back I can't believe what I see. A man, and a woman are in bed under blue blankets. Their brown skin looks ash grey, and a big yellow dog is lying on the bed at their feet. His pink tongue is hanging out of the side of his mouth. They are all dead.

I scream.

I faint.

# Chapter Sixteen

I'm awake now. I'm still lying down in the middle of the hallway though. In the doorway of the bedroom I saw the bodies, I see Marcy, Champagne and Dixon's ankles. I stand up slowly because I feel light headed.

From my position I can see the dead people again, and the smell is heavier than ever. But, Marcy and them don't appear to be bothered by the odor. Maybe they see this type of thing all of the time. I count the dead bodies in my mind that have occurred since I hooked up with them. Dragon. Joey. Peter. The Little girl. Maybe being around dead bodies is regular for them.

"Who are they?" Marcy asks Dixon.

"My parents," Dixon responds. "Don't bother them though, because they still sleeping. They need their rest."

Marcy looks at her, and pulls the gun out of her waist. "These mothafuckas ain't sleep, they dead. What are you some sort of sicko or something?"

"My family is sleep, and I'm not sick," Dixon says sternly. She walks into the room, and kisses them each on the forehead. She doesn't kiss the dog. I figure its because she doesn't like him. "They are in forever peace."

Marcy cocks her weapon, "Look, I don't know what kind of game you playing here, but I don't fuck around. What happened to them?"

"I told you already," she responds. "They are in forever sleep. They will be fine for the rest of their lives. No one will ever bother them, and they will never bother me."

"How did they bother you?" Champagne asks.

"The constant abuse," Dixon shakes her head and looks down at their bodies. "The constant calling me fat. I hate not being called by my name."

Me too. I think.

"I just couldn't take it anymore." She takes her fingers and stuffs them into her ears. "I can even hear them now. Can't you?"

"So what did you do to them?" Marcy frowns ignoring her question.

She takes her fingers out of her ears. "I poisoned their food," she fluffs the pillow behind the man's head. "A little at first, but more over time." She fluffs the woman's pillow.

"How the fuck did you get poison?" Marcy questions.

"My father works at a biology lab for pharmaceuticals. He has access to all sorts of things like that."

Marcy's eyes widen with pleasure. "Do you have more?"

Dixon laughs. "No, I gave them everything I had." She grins. "Besides, they deserved it."

"Well if you knew they were dead…,"

"Forever sleep," Dixon says cutting Champagne off. "Not dead."

"Well if you knew they were forever sleep, why did you say they were out of town?" Champagne continues. "It seems like you playing a bunch of games right now."

"Yeah…and the only games I like are the ones I start," Marcy says. "So what the fuck is going on around here for real?"

"They told you didn't they?" Dixon asks them both. "They told you about me?"

"Told you what?"

"That I'm a habitual liar?"

Marcy and Champagne look at each other. I look at all of them. At this point in the conversation I seem to be the only person who remembers that three funky corpses are on the bed.

"Wait, so you a liar?" Marcy asks stepping into the room.

"I knew something didn't add up with this bitch," Champagne says shaking her head. "I knew the moment I saw her face that something was up. I never thought she was a creep though."

"They think I'm a liar," Dixon responds. "But, I don't think so. I never thought so, that's why I didn't like going to the therapy."

Marcy points the gun at Dixon's head and pushes the barrel against her scalp. "Do you know Brillo or not, bitch? I have reached the end of my rope with you."

"Yes," she nods her head slowly. "Please don't shoot me."

"I'm not sure about what I plan to do with you yet," Marcy tells her. "It depends on if you lying or not about Brillo. Now, I need you to prove to me that you even know this nigga."

"What do you want me to do?"

"Show me proof," Marcy says. "Call him."

"I can't call him," Dixon replies. "He has his phone off."

"Well how we know you not habitually lying in this mothafucka right now?" Champagne asks her. "Because, to tell you the truth nothing about you seems real. We need proof, and we need it now."

As they watch Dixon, I watch them all. My shirt is hiked up over my nose to try and shield some of the smell of the bodies. It's not working though.

"I can show you some pictures," Dixon tells Champagne. "Will that work?"

When we make it to Dixon's room, and she opens the door I think we're all blown away. Everything seems neat in terms of furniture. In fact nothing is out of place. But, the walls are littered with pictures of Brillo. They are large pictures too. The size of a sheet of notebook paper.

"What is all of this?" Marcy asks stepping into the room looking all over the walls. "Some sort of shrine or something?"

"Don't touch anything," Dixon yells with an attitude. "Don't touch anything in my room." She pushes past Champagne, and me as we stand in the doorway. Our bodies are knocked into the edges of the door due to her hips. "Everything in here is perfect."

Marcy looks at Dixon, and snatches a picture off of the wall anyway. Dixon is enraged, and runs toward her. But, Marcy catches her with a blow to the temple using the butt of her gun. Dixon falls to the cream sheet on her bed.

"Pull that shit again, and you gonna get hit with something else," Marcy says to her. "Stay right there. And, don't move."

"What is this shit?" Champagne says entering the room.

I'm right behind her.

"I told you...pictures of my beloved," she says wiping the blood off of her head and onto her jeans.

"These aren't just pictures," Marcy says. "It looks like you stalking him. What are you some weird stalker chick?"

"How can I stalk somebody I love?" She asks with an attitude.

Champagne grabs a picture off of the wall. She holds it up. "This was taken the last day we saw Brillo. Where were you?"

"Around," she says. "I'm always around." She giggles to herself. "Brillo loves that about me."

When I observe all of Brillo's pictures on the wall suddenly I get warm inside. I can see how someone would want to stalk him. He's perfect. His smooth brown skin, and his wide eyes. They seem to be looking at me, and calling my name. Not the name Crystal that everyone wants me to go by. They are calling my real name. Porsche Shakur.

"Why are you taking all of these pictures if you all are together?" Marcy says, snatching picture after picture from the wall. I think she's trying to irritate her, by snatching the pictures down more than anything else.

"Because, I know he's worth a lot of money, and I worry about somebody kidnapping him for profit," Dixon responds. "I'm protecting him."

When she tries to stand up again Marcy says, "If you lift them thighs off of that bed you are as good as dead."

Dixon remains sitting down.

I take one picture off of the wall. It's a picture of Brillo and Crystal. Brillo doesn't seem happy in it. And, because Crystal and me look alike, it makes me feel like he isn't happy with me.

When Marcy pulls down a picture of herself, Champagne and Crystal she goes ballistic. She stuffs the barrel of the gun into Dixon's mouth and says, "I'm done fucking around with your sick ass," she yells. "Now do you know Brillo or not?"

We all crowd around the bed and wait for the answer.

"Yes, I know him," she says as best as she can with the barrel of the gun lying on her tongue. "And if you give him fifteen more minutes, you'll see for yourself."

An hour passes, and no Brillo. We are sitting in the living room, still surrounded by the odor of dead bodies. I want out of here. But, I know as mad as they are, that giving my two cents would make matters worse.

Marcy stands up and says, "That's it, I'm done with you."

She walks over to Dixon, and is about to shoot her. I cover my eyes and then there is a knock at the door.

"Who the fuck is that?" Marcy whispers with the gun still at Dixon's head. "You expecting company?"

"It's Brillo," she says. "I told you he was on his way. Do you believe me now? Or, am I still crazy in your eyes."

Marcy and Champagne lift her off the couch, and push her toward the door.

"Ask who is it," Marcy demands. "And, if you try to be slick I will open your head up in here like a raw egg, and kill whoever is at the door next."

"All that is unnecessary," Dixon says. "This is the person who you been waiting on."

The knock grows louder. And, I realize I'm biting my nails. All of this excitement is too much pressure for me.

"Bitch, I said ask who is at the door," Marcy says in a harsh whisper.

Dixon clears her throat, looks at the door and says, "Who is it?"

"It's me, baby," the man says. "Brillo. Open the door."

Marcy and Champagne's eyes widen.

"Now do you believe me?" Dixon asks them.

# Chapter Seventeen

The door hasn't even opened yet, but I can't stop smiling. Brillo is a rock star in my eyes. He is like the superstar you never get to meet, although you always wanted to. I'm trembling again, and it seems like it's taking forever for the door to finally open. But, when it does I'm thoroughly disappointed. I'm glaring.

The person on the other side looks the exact opposite of Brillo. He's tall, and has a frumpy body. His face is covered with black hair, and a thick pair of brown glasses rests against his nose. Who is this dude, because, he definitely isn't Brillo.

"Hey, baby," Brown Glasses, says to Dixon. "What took you so long to open the door?" He looks at all of us. "And, who are these people?"

"Your worst nightmares," Marcy says never missing an opportunity for drama. She raises the gun at him. "Now get your whack ass in here, before I blow the glasses off your face. And, do it quick too."

Brown Glasses runs into the apartment, but he's smiling. It's like he thinks it's a joke. Marcy closes and locks the door.

"Get over there on the couch. Both of you," Marcy says to Dixon and Brown Glasses.

They walk over to the couch and flop down. "Baby," Brown Glasses says to Dixon although he's looking at Marcy, "what's going on here?" He's still smiling. What's so funny? There is a gun at his head.

"How about you tell me what's going on here," Marcy says never taking the gun off of them. "Why are you in here pretending to be a nigga you couldn't come close to?"

His glasses fog up. They must irritate Marcy because she takes them off of his face; throws them on the floor, and stomps on them. The same way she did Dixon's glasses in the bathroom.

"Hey, why did you do that?" No Glasses asks. He's not smiling anymore. "Those things cost $200. Who is going to replace them? This is going too far now."

"You ain't answer the question yet," Marcy says. "Why are you in here pretending to be Brillo?"

"I thought we were in character," No Glasses says to her. He places his hand over his heart. "Don't you get it, I'm Brillo."

Marcy looks so angry she's breathing rapidly. I know something final is about to happen, but I don't know what. If No Glasses knew the kind of person she was he wouldn't play games like this.

"So you actually going to sit over there, and act like you a nigga who you not?" Champagne questions. "Do you think we would actually be in here doing all of this if we didn't know Brillo personally?"

"Leave him alone," Dixon says. "You're scaring him."

"What is wrong with you?" Marcy says looking down at her. "Do you think that we believe for a second that this ugly mothafucka is Brillo?"

"He is Brillo," Dixon says passionately. "What is wrong with you two?" She looks at me. "Can you help me? Please." Dixon asks me.

"I can't do nothing for you," I reply. The truth is I'm kind of irritated too. Maybe, it would be different if he looked something like Brillo. But, he so far off that it's not even funny. Fuck this dude.

"I'm going to ask you this one more time," Marcy says. "Why are you in here perpetrating a fraud?"

The room is filled with silence. I wonder if he'll come clean now, since it's obvious nobody here believes in him.

"I'm acting as Brillo," he says again.

Things get wild now. Marcy hits No Glasses in the head with the butt of her gun, but he quickly fights back. He grabs her, and pulls her onto his body. He hits her at least three times in the face, and stomach. The gun drops out of Marcy's hand. And, Dixon jumps out of the way, and stands against the wall next to me. Her hips brush against my thigh, and pushes me a little over.

Champagne runs over to them, and hits No Glasses in the back of the head. He turns around and grabs Champagne, and tries to choke the life out of her. Then he punches her in the stomach hard. At least that's what it looks like from where I'm standing anyway. But, the three of them are fighting so hard; that I know at least one of them will die. The only question is who, and how.

I wonder should I do something, and help the girls out. Something in me says no, and to let them battle it out their selves. I mean, it's not like we're friends. Marcy told me herself in her house. So why should I care what happens to them right now? They've killed people for no reason. They've held me hostage, and have not allowed me to go home. So maybe it is best if they die.

But, when I see him move for the gun, I grow nervous. Champagne is now lying on the black pillow on the floor, holding her stomach. She looks hurt pretty bad. Marcy on the other hand, looks like she could go about five more rounds.

I figure I should help her out. I just hope I don't regret this later. I rush toward the gun, pick it up, and hand it to Marcy. She points it into No Glasses' stomach, as he lies on top of her, and pulls the trigger. A shower of blood sprays into her face, and neck. She wipes it off, and pushes him off of her. His body makes a loud thump on the living room floor.

She stands up, and looks at me. Breathing heavily she says, "Good looking out, Crystal."

I regret my decision to help her already. After everything I just did, I still don't get to be called by my name.

Marcy aims the gun at Dixon. "Sit the fuck down before I shoot you too," she threatens.

Dixon hustles to the sofa, and plops down.

Marcy helps Champagne onto the recliner. "Are you okay?" She asks her.

"Yeah," Champagne responds in a low voice. "He hit me in the stomach pretty hard. I can barely breathe."

"You want to go to the hospital?" Marcy frowns. She looks worried about her.

"No," Champagne moans leaning on her side. "Just give me one of them beers out of the refrigerator. And, put some gin in it too. I'll be fine in about an hour." I guess she wants something stronger now.

Feeling useless, I quickly go fill her order, and hand her the drink.

"Thank you, Porsche," Champagne says to me. "I really appreciate what you did just now. That nigga could've killed all three of us."

This was the first time since I met Champagne that I felt good around her. She acknowledged what I did by calling me by my name. Something that Marcy didn't do. I smile, and sit back on the recliner.

"Don't move," Marcy says to Dixon again. "If you move an inch, I will shoot both of your eyes out. Am I clear?"

"Yes," she says raising her hands in the air. "You're clear."

Marcy takes her cell phone from her pocket, and makes a call. "Crys, why haven't you been answering the fucking phone? Do you know how much shit has gone on just now?"

Champagne sits straight up and looks at Marcy. "Put it on speaker phone," Champagne tells Marcy. "I want to talk to her too."

She does.

"I'm sorry, I just been going through it today," Crystal says. "I guess when ya'll called I couldn't get to the phone."

I hate that girl. She acts like she is some kind of queen. Why does she get to avoid a situation that involves her?

"Well we've gone through it too," Marcy tells her. "I just fought some nigga claiming to be Brillo."

"And, I just got my ass beat," Champagne yells from the sofa. "We almost died in here!"

"Now this chick does not know where Brillo is. So if she doesn't have him, where is he?" Marcy questions Crystal. "This shit is beyond old right now. I'm ready to be done with all this shit."

"I never said she had Brillo, or knew where he was," she says.

Marcy and Champagne give each other another facial expression. The only difference is that now Marcy is gritting her teeth.

"If Brillo isn't with this bitch, why are we even here?" Champagne asks. "This is ridiculous now."

"Ya'll can't be mad at me because you made assumptions," Crystal says. "I said bring her to me, and I would've asked her all of the questions I wanted to know."

"But you wouldn't answer your phone," Marcy screams. "How can anybody get a hold of you if you don't answer the phone? We've been here for hours trying to get a hold of you."

"Look, I can't stay on the phone. I gotta go," Crystal says. "I want one thing answered but I need proof. Since ya'll won't bring her here, find out if the bitch is HIV positive, and get back to me. Then, this will be all over soon."

Marcy hangs up the phone, and stuffs it into her pocket. She walks over to Dixon, and stares down at her. "Are you HIV-positive?"

We all look at her. The situation has taken on another turn.

"Yes, I am."

"Did you give it to Brillo?" Marcy questions.

"He may have given it to me," Dixon responds.

"Do you even know Brillo?" Marcy asks. "Not the nigga on this floor, but the real Brillo?"

"Yes," Dixon says.

"Then why are you pretending that this man is Brillo, when he isn't?" Champagne questions.

"Because, Brillo had sex with me once, and gave me HIV," she cries. "I love him so much that I needed to pretend that I was with him all the time. The person you killed agreed to play the game with me for a school project. I told him he needed to be Brillo no matter what. He likes me so he went all the way. Until you killed him."

"So why wouldn't he tell us who he really was when we pointed a gun at his nostrils?" Marcy asks.

"Because, he probably thought it was a part of the acting," she says. "It wasn't until you fought that he knew things were serious."

Marcy shakes her head and throws her body on the floor pillow. She rubs her temples. "I don't know what's going on, and why my friend wants to know your status. But tomorrow morning we are all going to the clinic. You are going to be tested for HIV. There's a place in Maryland that can let you know the preliminary results in one day, and the official results a few days later. If you aren't HIV positive you are dead. No more lies, and no more games. Okay?"

# SAD SUNDAY
# DAY FIVE
# Chapter Eighteen

We're sitting in a STD clinic. All of us. Side by side. Our backs are against a wall. Marcy is sitting next to Dixon, and we all are quiet.

A girl is looking at us across the room. Her weave looks choppy, and I hate looking at it. I wonder if she's staring at us, because she can see the gun Marcy has in the pit of Dixon's back. I got up five times, and walked back toward Marcy and Dixon, just to see if anybody can see anything if they are looking at us. No one could see a thing. But, it doesn't make my nerves relax.

"I have a question," Marcy says.

It was the first thing anybody said all morning. I was grateful that the silence was broken. I hate not knowing where a person is coming from, or what a person is thinking. Silence to me is worse than pain.

When no one responds Champagne says, "Whom was your question directed to? You got to be more specific. Four mothafuckas are over here."

Marcy looks at Dixon. "She knows who I'm talking to. Don't you, Dixon? She's not dumb. Are you, Dixon?"

Dixon wipes sweat off of her forehead. "I'm not dumb. But, I don't know what you want to ask me. I told you everything you wanted to know already."

"Not everything," Marcy says. "There are still some questions out there." She taps her foot on the floor.

"So what do you want to know now?" Dixon swallows.

"If it is true, that you know Brillo, where did you meet him?" Marcy looks at Dixon from her feet to her hair. "It doesn't add up," she shrugs. "But, maybe it never will."

"I met him at the gas station," Dixon replies wiping the sweat off of her cheeks. "I was getting something for my mother, and he walked up to me. Said I was pretty. Not the kind of pretty that's manufactured, or anything like that. He said I had natural beauty."

Champagne and Marcy burst into laughter. And, since things have been tense all day, I was grateful.

"You know what," Marcy says. "The more you talk, the more I realize how big of a liar you are. And, it will be my pleasure to kill you when it's all said and done. I don't get a lot of pleasure these days, so you have to believe me when I say I'm looking forward to this shit. Taking your life will be the ultimate orgasm."

"Why is it so hard for you to believe that someone could be attracted to me just the way that I am?"

"Because you don't even believe it yourself," Marcy replies. "You're insecure. If you weren't you wouldn't feel the need to have sex with someone else's man."

Dixon frowns. She rotates her head so that she's looking directly into Marcy's eyes. She doesn't say anything for a second. So the tension is thicker now.

"I told you one million times already, so I'm sorry if you're not listening, but Brillo belongs to me," Dixon says strongly. "Even if he didn't believe it, or knew it at the time. We are meant to be, and one day he'll come to his senses. It may not be today, and it may not be tomorrow, but it will be soon. And, then you can eat your words." Dixon laughs. "I'll even invite you to our wedding. It will be the event of the century," Dixon says looking into the ceiling. "As a matter of fact you all are invited." She looks at us.

"There will be an event, but it won't be no wedding," Marcy says. "I don't know what happened to you in your life, but the good thing is I'm getting ready to put you out of your misery."

"Is Ms. Terry here?" A young black nurse asks.

We all stand up. Marcy stuffs her gun into the back of her shirt, and pulls it down to cover it. But, she still has a grip on Dixon's chubby arm.

We all walk toward the nurse. We stand behind Dixon like we are her entourage. For the moment, I guess we are.

"Only one visitor per patient," the nurse says to us.

"It's okay, they can come in with me," Dixon tells her.

I'm surprised she's so cooperative. Maybe she is HIV positive. Maybe she isn't lying after all.

"You don't understand, it's not safe for the doctor or for the patient," the nurse continues.

"And, you don't understand," Marcy says. "Now we are coming with her. So don't make a problem for yourself when their ain't one. This is just a job. Don't be a hero. Okay?"

The nurse seems nervous. I guess she never met a pretty beast before.

"Well, I guess it will be okay," the nurse replies clearing her throat. "But, if the doctor says you all have to leave, there is nothing I can do about it."

"We'll just deal with him like we dealing with you, when that time comes," Marcy responds.

The nurse seems more nervous now. I know the feeling. "Okay, well, right this way."

We follow her to an office way in the back of the clinic. She opens the door and we all pile inside. "You can sit on the table," she says to Dixon. "Where you were earlier to-day."

"I have to take off my clothes again for the doctor?" Dixons asks with wide eyes. "I don't mind if I have too."

"No," the nurse shakes her head. "There's no need to do that. The doctor already gave you a pelvic exam."

"I know, but I don't mind if he does it again," Dixon says smiling crazily. "It didn't hurt at all. Like I thought it would anyway."

"Uh…it's quite alright," the nurse says holding her hand out. "We got all of the tests we need on you."

Dixon seems disappointed and the nurse leaves the room in a strange mood.

"What are you some kind of strange freak?" Marcy asks. "The woman said they had everything they needed."

"I'm not a freak," Dixon responds. "I'm just trying to be helpful. So that y'all can have everything you need, and leave me alone."

"Yeah, but the nurse said he looked at your pussy already," Champagne adds. "You acted like you wanted him to go another round."

Champagne sits in one seat, and Marcy sits in the other. Which, means I'm the only one left standing, because their ain't no more seats.

"You don't have to use those words," Dixon says. "Those nasty words like pussy. I don't like them. They aren't lady-like."

"Just sit the fuck back and be quiet," Marcy says. "I'm tired of hearing your voice."

As we wait for the doctor, Champagne takes her cell phone out of her pocket, and makes another call. She's been calling somebody all day, but nobody seems to answer. Her mood is changing, and I start to feel sorry for her. She's not as mean, and as crazy as Marcy now. She just seems to be caught up in her sorrow. I think she really misses her family.

"My mother still isn't answering the phone," Champagne says to Marcy putting the phone into her purse. "When we leave out of here I gotta go check on my people."

"I don't think that's a good idea," Marcy says to her. "I know you're worried, but you don't have to…"

"I haven't spoken to my family all day," Champagne yells hitting her leg. "It is unlike my mother not to call me at least once. Do you think he—,"

"Don't even think like that," Marcy says cutting her off. "The only thing on our minds should be finding out if this bitch is HIV-positive or not. The moment we get the information, will be the moment we can put this all behind us, and find Brillo."

"But what if Axe did hurt my family?"

"Then you still have me," Marcy replies.

When the doctor finally comes into the office he looks at us strangely. "Well, it seems like I have a big audience today."

Crickets.

He clears his throat and says to Dixon, "Well young lady, I have some great news." He pauses, "and, lately that has not been the case. You wouldn't believe how many young girls lives are changed forever when they leave my office."

"Don't flatter yourself, doctor," Marcy says. "Just the results please."

"Okay," he adjusts the papers in his hand. "You are HIV negative. In fact, you never had sex. When I first gave you a pelvic exam I was able to see that your hymen was still in tact. I can't remember the last time I saw a hymen," he laughs.

"So you lied?" Marcy questions Dixon with a major attitude. "All of the games for nothing? You don't even know what a dick is?"

"Is everything okay here?" The doctor asks. He opens the door, and a blast of cool air rolls inside. "I'm feeling a lot of tension in this room. We just heard some good news. Everyone should be happy now."

Marcy ignores him and says, "Why the games, Dixon? Why waste everybody's time?"

"Because I don't have a life," she says under her breath. "And I wanted a life. I wanted Crystal's."

"It's time to go," Marcy says standing up grabbing Dixon by the arm, and moving toward the door.

It's like the doctor isn't even there anymore. He's being totally ignored by everybody, including me.

The moment we walk into the hall, I know Dixon's life is about to be over, until we see a police officer.

Dixon breaks away from us, and runs toward him.

Oh shit! She's going to tell the cops and now we all will be in trouble.

# MEAN MONDAY
# DAY SIX
# Chapter Nineteen

I'm sitting in the backseat thinking about my dirty clothes. I'm wearing the same ones I had on the first day Champagne got me. I need to change. Marcy and Champagne have changed everyday. I guess Champagne was right, it pays to keep fresh clothing with you at all times.

Champagne and I are in the car, and Marcy is outside. She's talking on the phone to somebody. She does a lot of that, talking on the phone away from us.

I don't trust Marcy. And, it's not because of the obvious, that she's a killer, and selfish. I don't trust her, because if you aren't loyal to your friends, you won't be loyal to anyone else, and, that includes strangers.

I'm thinking of my mother again, and how I miss her more when I hear Champagne. She's in the driver's seat crying.

"You can leave today," she tells me looking at me through the rearview mirror. She's crying. "You can go back home if you want too. I'm not holding you hostage anymore."

I would be lying if I didn't say I was a little relieved. But, I also feel sad. I know now that although I want to go home, I don't want to return to my old life. I'm going home to nothing. Something about not knowing what will happen each day is exciting.

"Thank you," I say under my breath. "But, are you okay?"

"Like you care," she says to me wiping her eyes with the back of her hand. Her black mascara smears all over her cheeks, and under her eyes. "You probably are happy that I'm like this."

I should be, but I'm not. "Why you say that?"

"Because of everything I've done to you," she says under her breath. "Taking you away from your family, and forcing you to be around us." She shakes her head. "I'm awful, and, I'm going to get what I deserve. I don't know when, but I know it will be soon."

I move a little in my seat. "Don't talk like that," I say. "You don't deserve anything bad to happen to you."

"Yes I do," she looks at Marcy outside. "All of my friends do. But, not you." She turns around and looks at me. "We've robbed people. We've murdered people. And, we've set people up for big sums of money. But, you are different. You're innocent. You don't get to live a life like the one I led, and not pay with your heart sooner or later."

Her confession shocks me. "Why do you do those things?" I run my hands over my knees to give them something to do. I wasn't expecting the confession from her. "If you are sad about it, just do right by people."

"I'm not sad about doing dirty," she says to me sipping the sweet vodka in her bag. It's then that I realize I want some liquor. Again, she must be reading my mind because she hands it to me. "I'm sad about what's to come. I'm expecting my karma any day now."

I take a big gulp and motion to hand it back. "Take some more," she says. "It's not Long Island Ice Tea, but it will make you feel good."

I take a larger sip. "So, what are you going to do now?" I ask. "With Dixon gone, will that be enough for Crystal to come back home? And, face Axe on her own?"

When we were at the clinic, Dixon ran to the police officer and told him she lost her glasses. Said she needed help outside to flag down a cab, because she couldn't see. He saw her all the way outside and into a cab. You should've seen Marcy's face as Dixon looked back at her and grinned. Marcy was mad, but I don't think it was because Dixon ran to the officer for help. I think it was, because she didn't get a chance to kill her. Marcy loves to murder. I can feel it in my heart.

Champagne laughs to herself. "Let me tell you something, and this is some real shit. You will always be as good as your friends." She turns around in the seat and looks at Marcy outside again. "If you selfish, how can you think that you'll have unselfish friends? It doesn't make logical sense. Crystal doing a lot of things, but she not facing Axe. She leaving that shit to me."

"Then why don't you get new friends?" I ask handing her back the bottle.

"Because, no one else will have me," she says crying harder. "I'm a fucking mess. I don't even want to be around myself half the time. How can I expect anybody else too?" She shakes her head. "Naw, I'm getting exactly what I deserve."

"Do you think Dixon will tell anybody that Marcy killed the fake Brillo?" I ask since she's in the talking mood.

"Only if she plans to tell them that she killed her parents, and the dog too," Champagne replies. "That's the only reason Marcy didn't care about going back to her house to put a bullet in her head. She's a murderer too. And murderers very rarely talk."

"So what are you going to do when you go home?" Champagne asks turning the bottle upside down to her lips.

"I know you're going to celebrate. Probably go see some of your friends."

"I know after hanging around me you probably think I'm some popular girl," I laugh. "But, I don't have many friends." I don't have any friends.

"It's hard for me to believe that," she says. "You're a really nice person. And, nice people are always surrounded by other nice people."

I look at Marcy outside. She has a grin on her face, and she's looking at me. I wonder who's on that phone.

"People don't like to hang out with you, when you don't know who you are," I say to Champagne. "People like to be around strong, and confident people. That's not me. Well," I pause, "that wasn't me. I feel like I can do anything now. Who knows what the future will hold for me. Before just now, when you told me I could go home, I thought I wouldn't live to see my 18th birthday."

She laughs. "You'll be fine."

"Since I got almost $1000 in my pocket, maybe I'll go to the store and get some new clothes. Maybe I'll start all over with my life." I shrug. "Who knows? What about you? What are your plans?"

She's quiet again. Did I already say that I hate when she does that?

"Do you remember in the IHOP restaurant what I told you?"

"To tell you the truth that time was blurry," I say. "I can't remember a lot about it. Just that I wanted to go home."

"Well you should always remember what somebody says to you," Champagne says. "Especially if the person has control over your life."

She's speaking in circles again. Maybe, she'll come around in a minute, and tell me what's really on her mind.

"I said with answers come great responsibilities," Champagne continues. "And, with great responsibility come greater risks. So do you still want to know?"

"No that's okay. I'm good."

She giggles and says, "That's what you said last time too." She laughs a little harder. "Hey, Porsche, thanks for making me smile."

Marcy finally walks back to the car, and gets inside. She looks back at me, and grins again. Why does she keep doing that?

"So what was that all about?" Champagne asks Marcy. "You were on the phone an awful long time. Is everything cool?"

"Couldn't be better, my friend," Marcy responds clapping her hands together. "But, I have a question for you."

"Shoot," Champagne says.

"If we had to put Crystal out there to save ourselves, would you be willing to do it?"

"What are you talking about?" Champagne frowns. "Crystal is our bitch. And, she may be doing the most right now, but she's still our friend. She'll come around."

"You can't worry about her," Marcy says. "You should worry about yourself. Besides, Crystal has given us her ass to kiss. And, I'm tired of not being paid for my services with trying to help her get out of this shit. I'm starting to think about me now."

"You know what," Champagne says. "I don't even want to talk about it anymore. All I want to do is go see my family. And, can't nobody stop me."

You ever see one of them murder movies, where twenty something cop cars are out front of a house, that's surrounded by yellow tape? Well that's the scene we ran into, when we pulled up in front of Champagne's house.

"Oh my God," Champagne screams and parks the car. She covers her mouth with both hands. "What is going on?"

"Maybe it's not that bad," Marcy says looking just as horrified. "We can't go in though, because you know we got papers on us."

Champagne is already out of the car before Marcy can dispute. And, since she took the car keys with her, we are stuck. We both get out too. There is so much going on outside, that we were able to slip past the officers and into the house without being spotted.

The moment we open the back door I can smell the scent of gunpowder in the air. I know the odor too well, since I've been around Marcy.

I don't go any further, because the first thing I see stops my heart. Marcy and Champagne disappear into the rest of the house.

The thing I see on the floor, under the kitchen table, calls my attention. I get on my knees, and pull it out. It's sticky grey and red. I know what it is now. It's a bloodied Brillo pad. Somebody was sending a message. And, I think I know who.

# MEAN MONDAY

## DAY SIX

## Chapter Twenty

I'm riding in the back of a yellow cab. My hands are clasped together in my lap. My nerves are bad these days. I've seen more than I think any girl my age should see.

I had to get out of there. I had to get out of Champagne's house. I couldn't stand to hear her cries anymore, when she learned what happened to her family from one of her neighbors. She sounded like her heart had been pulled out of her chest and stomped on. Maybe it had. He left her home a bloody mess.

Axe murdered the two people Champagne seemed to care about the most. Her mother, and her goddaughter who was over the house visiting. I know Axe wants to find his brother Brillo, but I can't understand how hurting innocent people will help him achieve his goal.

The saddest part was, since Champagne has warrants out for her arrest, she couldn't talk to the cops. I think they are looking for her now. I think they want to make sure she isn't responsible for the murder of her own family.

Now that I am free to go home, I took advantage by getting out of that house as fast as I could.

I lean forward in the backseat. "You can let me out right here," I tell the cab driver.

I'm a few blocks away from my building. I want to go into *Eazy's Liquor* store to buy a cream soda, and a bag of cheese Doritos, before I go into the house.

As he brings the car to a slow drive, I ease into the middle of the back seat, and look at my face through the rear-view mirror. I look a wreck, but still better than what I looked when I was on this block six days ago.

"Ten dollars," the cab driver tells me, holding out his hand.

I dig into my pocket and separate a twenty-dollar bill from the pussy stack I earned in my pocket. "Keep the change," I tell him, which is something I never said before.

He smiles at me, and I hop out of the car. The sun is bright, but is not as hot as it usually is. And, surprisingly my block seems empty. I wonder where everyone is today.

I go into the store, and buy what I want. When I come out I run into Chris. The boy I let finger fuck me in his mother's truck a few weeks ago. He's wearing the same yellow shirt I saw him in the last time I was out here. I know I can't say much, sense I'm still wearing the same pink polo shirt, and blue True Religion jeans that Champagne gave me when she scooped me up, but still I expect more from him.

"Damn, Twin," Chris says walking up behind me. "Damn, you look good. What you do, come up on some money or something?"

I twist the top off of my soda, and throw the cap on the ground. I hate the sound of Chris' voice. And, now that I think of it, I should've never given him the time of day. It's too late now.

"I'm busy," I tell him walking to my building taking a big sip.

"Can I have some?" He asks looking at my body.

"Not a chance," I respond sipping some more soda.

"I'm talking about the chips," he replies looking at my hand.

"You can't have shit over here," I tell him seriously. "So turn your eyes away."

He chuckles. "Did you hear about what happened to your uncle?" He asks walking up behind me. "They beat him real bad the last time I saw you. His head was busted open, and everything. The nigga needed like fifty stitches to put his face back together. Maybe, now he'll learn to leave them young girls alone."

I shrug like I could care less, although my heart breaks. I love my uncle. I probably always will. I just can't understand why he has to be the way that he is.

"My uncle is a grown man," I respond drinking the rest of my soda and throwing the plastic bottle on the ground. "That's on him. I gotta worry about me."

"You cold hearted now," he says to me. "Why you gotta be that way?"

I stop walking, and spin around on my heels to look into his face. I still can't believe I thought he was so cute at one point and time. He's young, and broke and could never stand next to a man like Brillo.

I feel gut punched when I realize that since I'm going home today, I'll never be able to meet him in person. I won't know if he's dead or alive. I won't know if they'll find him. I won't know if he would've ever given a girl like me a chance.

I rub my pocket because stuffed inside of it, is the picture of him and Crystal that I stole from Dixon's house. I look at it whenever I'm in the bathroom alone, so that no one will know that I have it. The more I stare at his photo, the more I convince myself that he could be mine. Geez. I sound as crazy as Dixon.

"I'm not being no kind of way," I say to Chris. "You just not the kind of nigga I fuck with anymore. You ain't got enough money for me, or nothing. I'm sorry."

His eyebrows rise. "So what are you, some kind of whore or something?" he asks me. "Because, don't even act like I didn't hit that pussy for free already. You can't put a price tag on something you take out of the trash can."

I feel like punching him in the face, but I won't. "Look, it ain't about being a whore, it's about getting your worth," I tell him. "You don't have no money so you can't do nothing for me. Just be glad you got a whiff of this pussy when you did. That's all I can say." I walk on the first step leading into my building.

"Wait," he yells to me. "If I want to spend some time with you now, how much would it cost?"

I think its funny how the same nigga who was giving me face six days ago is now worried about what's between my legs. And, even though I don't need his money, because I got a nice stack in my pocket, I decide to see where his head is at.

"One hundred dollars," I tell him. "And, don't tell me you don't have it because I already know that you don't."

He looks embarrassed, and I try to hide my smile.

"How you know I don't have it?" Chris asks.

"Because you still ain't show me shit yet," I respond. "And, I'm not trying to hear none of that shit you be spitting, about you gonna get me later. It's money now or never in this game. So what you gonna do?"

I can't believe my eyes when he digs into his pocket. He pulls out a small stack. Since I know now what it feels like to be in the possession of a thousand dollars, I figure he's holding about four hundred dollars in his hand.

"Here," he says handing me a one hundred dollar bill. "Now what you gonna say?"

I smile, and stuff the money into my pocket. "Damn, I can't even lie, you fooled the hell out of me."

"See, you better recognize," he says popping his dingy collar. "Around here I gets money."

"That's good for you," I grin. "I'm very proud of you, Chris. But, look, I'm going to go into the house and see about my mother. And, when I'm done I'm gonna come back out here. Where you want me to meet you?"

"You can meet me at my house," he tells me. "My mother not gonna be home all day. She going to some church event or something."

"Okay, I'll be right there," I tell him holding his hand. "And, keep that thing hard for me." I rub his dick in his jeans, which feels like a small finger. "Because, I'm gonna fuck you all night." I push the bag of chips into his chest. "You can have these, they are on me."

He takes the bag, and smiles all the way up the block. I watch him the entire way. Stupid ass nigga. I wish I would meet him anywhere. He lost it with me. After the way he did me with the Happy Meal thing, this money is as good as gone.

When I pull the door open to my building and walk in, my old neighbor Sally is walking out of the door. Her hair is littered with pink rollers, and she's rocking a holey red housecoat. "Porsche, where have you been?" She asks me like she got the right to. "You almost gave your mother a heart attack."

"I been around," I say walking toward the steps.

She grabs me by my wrists. "Don't get sassy with Ms. Sally," she yells. "I don't play that old disrespectful bullshit you kids of the day be throwing your parents. Now I asked you where you been, and I expect an answer."

I snatch my arm away from her, and rub the area her nails dug into my skin. "Listen, Ms. Sally, I don't have to tell you shit about my life. If my mother wants to question me about my whereabouts when I get into the house, then she's welcome to it. But, you not my mother," I say stabbing my finger into her soft titty, "so you can just back the fuck off."

I turn around to walk away.

"Well I never," she says as I stomp up the stairs.

I open the door with the key under the mat and walk inside my house. My mother is not here. I'm not surprised though. She's probably on the street somewhere hanging out with the rest of her drunk friends.

I go into my bedroom. It feels so good to be here, although its not the best room in the world. I don't have a lot of frills. Just a twin bed, a small grey TV, and pictures of Usher over my wall.

I take Brillo's picture out of my pocket and set it on the dresser. I stare at it while I take my clothes off. I look for something clean to wear. I want to hop into my red tracksuit, but I can't find it anywhere. So I settle on some jeans, and a lavender shirt instead. Then I grab some white cotton panties. They're ugly and have a hole in the butt part. That's one of the things I want to do when I spend my money, buy all new underwear. I want to feel sexy from now on, like a girl.

I hop into the shower, and put my fresh clothes on. Then I take the red Chi flat iron from up under the sink, and iron my hair. I don't look as pretty as I did when I first got my bob done, but I still look better than before I left the block.

After unplugging the flat iron, I open the bathroom door to walk, and run right into my mother. She's wearing the red tracksuit I was looking for, and she looks pretty in it. Her long black hair is pulled into a ponytail, and she has no makeup on her yellow face.

Before I can say hello, she pulls me into her arms and hugs me tightly. I don't know why, but suddenly I start crying. I'm not talking about a little cry. I'm talking about the kind of cry that hurts your tummy, and makes you feel like you been doing sit-ups all day.

When she's done she pushes me back, and says, "Where have you been, Porsche? I have been worried sick."

"I ran away," I tell her.

We walk into the living room. She sits on the black leather recliner, and I sit on the black couch across from her. I sit on the part of the couch that doesn't sink to the floor like quicksand. This apartment is old as shit like Dixon's place. Nothing new and pretty is in here like the stuff Marcy has at her house.

"Why did you do that?" She asks me. "I was a mess. I called the police, your school, and even that one girl I saw you hang out with before in this building."

"She's not my friend, ma," I say embarrassed. "I just sit at the bus stop with her. The only thing she says to me is do I know what time the bus is gonna get here."

"Well I asked her and she didn't know where you were."

I'm mad. "Why did you do that?"

"Because, I was scared."

I look around. I notice I don't see drink glasses lying all over the place. "Ma, have you been drinking?"

"No," she says. "I needed my mind together. I needed to think straight," she responds. I can see her body shaking. She does it a lot, just like me. "I won't be drinking no more at all."

She is crying now and I cry too. I want to stop though. My tummy still hurts from the last cry.

"Ma, please stop crying," I beg her.

"I can't," she says. "Porsche, I'm sorry about everything that I've done to you. I know it hasn't been an easy life, having to move all the time, but it was all I knew."

"Ma, do I have any relatives who look just like me?"

I don't know where the question came from. I don't remember being prepared to ask her. But, the question came out and now I want an answer.

Her eyes widen. "What your uncle tell you?" She asks glaring at me. "What did he say?"

My eyebrows rise. "Nothing...but...why are you acting like that?"

"You know what, you should've stayed your funky ass out there on them streets. I don't need none of this shit from you, Porsche! I'm grown. I'm your mother, you not mine," she yells as she goes to the kitchen cabinet to pour her some fruity vodka.

I guess she's off the wagon already.

"Just get out," she points. "I don't want to see you anymore. I hope you die." She walks to her room.

I stay where I am and cry. I don't know what just happened. Why would she wish something like that on me? Don't she know that God grants the wishes of a mother with a broken heart?

I get up to walk to go outside. I got to get some air. The moment I open the door, I'm pulled out of the apartment, and punched in the eye by Marcy.

At least somebody wants me.

# Chapter Twenty-One

When I wake up, I'm lying on the back seat of the Benz with a cold steak on my right eye. I guess somebody felt bad about my face, and put it on me.

As much as I don't like Marcy and Champagne, to be honest, I'm glad they came back for me. I just wish they would've asked me to stay, instead of hitting me. I would've said yes.

I realize I hate being home, and I hate being around my mother. She doesn't deserve my love and she doesn't deserve me. What caused her to get so mad when I asked if I had any relatives who look like me? Now I gotta know. I gotta ask Crystal. Maybe, she knows something I don't.

I'm about to sit up when I hear Marcy and Champagne whispering…about me.

"Look, I like her," Champagne says to Marcy. "What you did back there was wrong. You didn't have to hit her in the face."

"I'm sorry if you think my tactics were a little bit rough, but I can't let her get away right now," Marcy responds. "I need to make sure I can trust her first. I'm just looking out for us."

"But, I told her she could go home," Champagne says. "And, you treated her like she was some random bitch."

"Just because you started liking the chick doesn't mean she still ain't random," Marcy responds. "In the midst of all of this shit, don't forget who your real friends are, because I haven't. And, one day you gonna thank me."

"I can't live like this no more," Champagne sobs. "Axe took everything from me today. I don't have anything left. I feel like if we weren't doing the things that we were doing on the streets, none of this would've happened."

"Maybe you're right," Marcy replies. "But, we can't turn back now. We got to deal with this shit head on. And, you can't make no more decisions without involving me. Telling that girl she could leave was dumb. Had I not asked around where that girl lived, who knows who she may have told. We killed people in front of her. Don't you remember that?"

Now I'm really frightened. Scared murderers kill witnesses.

"She not telling nobody," Champagne says still crying. "And, I don't feel like talking about this right now. I got other shit on my mind," she sobs harder. "I…I can't believe."

"Let me drive," Marcy says when the car starts swerving. "You shouldn't be operating no vehicle like this anyway."

The car slows down, and one car door opens and closes, followed by the other. I keep my eye closed since the other one is covered with beef.

When the car starts again, I remain stiff. I want them to continue to talk. I want to see what dastardly plans they have in store for me now. I'm the kind of girl who rides rollercoasters with her eyes open. I like to know what's coming, whether I'm scared or not.

I'm waiting to ear hustle when all of a sudden I hear Marcy ask, "You up back there, Crystal?" She's calling me by the chick's name again. "If you are I'm sorry about what happened. I ain't mean to hit you in the eye so hard."

I remain silent. Besides, it would look fake to answer her immediately, because they will think I was up the entire time, and heard everything.

"Leave that girl alone," Champagne cries before blowing her nose. "She's probably still sleep."

"Well she needs to get the fuck up," Marcy says with an attitude. "Hey, Crystal, wake the fuck up! This ain't no train, and I'm not your personal driver."

"She might wake up if you call her by her fucking name for a change," Champagne replies. "Damn, you just love being disrespectful."

"How long are you going to be like this?" Marcy asks her.

"By be like this do you mean, how long am I going to grieve over my family?" Champagne asks with an attitude. "Because, I'm so sorry that my sorrow is getting on your nerves. Please forgive me for having feelings."

"I'm not saying all that," Marcy responds. "I'm just saying you still got me. Yet you over there acting like you don't have a friend in the world."

Finally I sit up and yawn. The steak on my eye falls off of my hand, and drops on top of my sneaker. I kick it away. When I look out of the window I see that we are in New York. Since I've been their hostage I've seen more of the east coast than I have my entire life.

"Glad you could get up," Marcy says looking at me from the rearview mirror. "And I'm sorry about your eye."

If she's so sorry, why is she smiling?

When I lean over, and look at it through the mirror I think I'm going crazy. It's totally black, and puffed out. "Oh my God," I yell touching it softly. "My face. Why did you do that?"

"I said I'm sorry," Marcy says dryly. "But, I ain't about to suck your clit."

I frown.

"I didn't know about the arrangement you made with Champagne," Marcy continues. "Right now we all got to stick together, okay? So you can't leave yet. Besides, I'm becoming attached to you. It ain't like we treated you so badly now is it?"

I think about the gun Brillo's sister pointed at my head. I think about how Champagne screamed in my face when I came behind her while she was talking to her father in the car. I think about the married couple, and the kid Marcy killed. I think about No Glasses that Marcy murdered in cold blood.

"No, Marcy," I say sarcastically, "hanging out with you has been a dream."

She laughs, and we pull in front of a strip club in New York called *Kitty Kats*. Marcy opens the glove compartment, and grabs some large black dark shades. She throws them back to me and says, "Put these on. I don't want nobody to know that we beat you."

She's laughing, but I'm pouting. I slide them on my face.

"Are you okay?" Marcy asks Champagne. "Because, we gotta go in there, and get some money. At the rate we going we won't have enough cash to pay next month's bills."

"With my mother, and goddaughter being dead, nothing else matters to me," Champagne responds wiping her nose with a light blue piece of crumbled Kleenex tissue.

"Well pull yourself together anyway," Marcy says drinking out of the small paper bag shaped like a bottle between her thighs. "You know Monday's at Kitty Kats are the best nights for us." Marcy grabs the other paper bag stuffed between Champagne's legs. "Here, sip this." Champagne does. "Drink more." Champagne drinks the entire bottle. "That's Marcy's little girl."

Marcy pops the trunk, and grabs two bags. Eventually we all make it into the club. It's dark, and crowded. I've never been to a strip club before, and suddenly I feel grown. I mean I was at *Three Girls Swingers* club, but that don't count. That place stank and was weird.

The first thing I do when I walk inside is go to the bar. I pull a twenty-dollar bill out of my pocket, and slap it on the brown wood. "I'll have a Long Island Ice Tea please," I say to the bartender.

"You can have a long walk up out of my face," the ugly bartender says to me while wiping the counter with a white rag. "I don't serve minors."

"Well do you serve pussy?" Marcy asks coming behind me.

Marcy leans against my back. Her titties are pressed against me, and the bar is digging into my stomach. Then she wraps her arms around me, raises my shirt and pinches my titties. I'm not much on girl-on-girl action, but I got to admit, I love the performance, and the look in his eyes.

The bartender smiles, and shakes his head. "You should've told me she was with you," he pushes my money back. "Any friend of Marcy's is a friend of mine."

I stuff the money back in my pocket, and wait on my drink.

"You stay right here," Marcy says pointing at me. "Me and Champagne got work to do. Be good, and don't get into no trouble. More than anything, don't leave."

Since Ugly Bartender leads me to believe that the drinks are free. I have no intentions on going anywhere.

When I get my first drink I turn around, and take a better look at the club. It's small and dark, but packed with men. In the back of the spot is a long stage that runs up the middle of the club. When I see Marcy and Champagne come out wearing matching hot pink sequin bras and thongs, my jaw drops. Their faces are painted extra, and they look so sexy, and pretty.

Champagne struts toward a silver pole that runs from the ceiling to the sage. She crawls all the way to the top like a monkey climbing a tree. Marcy crawls under her on the same pole, and with no hands, bends all the way back. Marcy's thighs are the only things holding her up on the pole. How did she do that?

With her hands free, Marcy takes Champagne's pink thongs off, and throws it into the pack of wild men. They are screaming and going wild. Then Marcy licks Champagne's pussy, while Champagne grinds her face. They are doing all of this while on the same pole. Out of nowhere, money starts falling from heaven. There is so much money in the air, that for a second I can't see them. All I see is green.

When I see all of the money they are making, I'm inspired to do my thing too. They didn't ask me, but if they bought me here it must be for a reason. They want me to get some cash too. With the drink in my cup all gone, I know it's time to do my thing.

So I ease out of my jeans, and fold them up on the bar stool. I still got my cotton panties with the hole in the butt on, until a strange man behind me eases them down my ankles. I kick them into the middle of the floor, put my hands on my knees and wiggle my naked bottom by the bar stool. Marcy and Champagne not the only mothafuckas about to make a little extra change.

I got me fifteen bucks already when all of a sudden I hear Ugly Bartender yell, "White Night, nooooooo!"

His voice sounds like he's trying to warn somebody to get out of the middle of the street, before they get ran over by a bus.

When I look behind me I see this six foot four inch white girl with black eye shadow and black lipstick rushing in my direction. Her body is in shape, but she's as thick as Ray Lewis.

I run toward the back of the club, and into a man looking at Champagne and Marcy on the stage. White Night, grabs my bob, and pulls me to her. Then she punches me in the face. I fall on the dirty floor and she stabs me in my right ass cheek with something hard.

I scream at the top of my lungs. And, when I look up at Marcy and Champagne on the stage, they look beyond mad with me.

I guess working the sidelines is frowned upon in this establishment.

"I hope you know you fucked it up for us tonight," Marcy says to me, while I'm sitting in the back seat. She's driving down the road. "Thanks to you, we not allowed in *Kitty Kats* no more. Some niggas said we not even allowed back in New York." She looks at my shades through the rearview mirror. "And, just so you know we hit that spot up once a week. I'm talking about we got paid three thousand a night there. You fucked all of that up, and gonna have to figure out a way to repay us."

Since they couldn't find my pants, with my money inside, the only thing on my ass right now is a band-aid they got from Rite Aid. I'm naked from the waist down. I know they could've gotten me something to put on. With all the shit they keep in the trunk, but they refuse. *Please God let me come on my period, and bleed all over these seats.* That'll show 'em.

"I'm sorry," I say feeling stupid. It's hard to feel good about yourself when you're wearing dark shades, a lavender shirt and no pants or panties. "All I wanted to do was make money like ya'll."

"Leave her alone," Champagne says. "She made a mistake. Besides, how many mistakes have you made?"

"Did you call Crystal again?" Marcy asks Champagne with an attitude.

"Yep, and she not answering the phone again," Champagne responds shaking her head. "I can't wait to get my hands on her. I'm telling you now I might kill her."

# Tell All Tuesday
# Day Seven
# Chapter Twenty-Two

We are sitting in the parking lot of a bowling alley in New York. Champagne had an emotional break down. She was driving when it happened. It was so bad that Marcy had to drive. But, when Champagne started punching at the air, and almost hit her, Marcy decided to pull over.

Champagne kept saying her mother was gone. I want to do more than sit back here. I really do feel bad for her loss. But, I get the impression that she still doesn't consider me a real friend. So I bite my tongue.

I try to get comfortable in the backseat, but my ass is sore, and my eye his throbbing. They bought me new clothes since my jeans were stolen, and I am officially broke.

Something about the way Marcy kept telling me she wanted to punch me in the other eye, while we were in the store, makes me think she isn't happy about spending so much money on me. But, somebody stole my money, and clothes. However, thanks to Marcy, I'm now the proud owner of two pairs of True Religion jeans, and three cute Gucci tops. I'm wearing my brown one today. Now I got stuff in the trunk of the Benz too. Does that make me official?

"Champagne, what can I do?" Marcy asks in a soft voice. "How can I make you feel better?" She places a hand on her shoulder. "Tell me? I'll do anything."

"Bring my mother back," Champagne says from the passenger seat. "Bring my goddaughter back too. You can start there."

"I can't do that," Marcy sighs rubbing her leg. "I wish I could."

"Well you can't do anything for me," Champagne continues rubbing her head. "I…don't know what to do anymore, Marcy. What's the use of getting money if you can't spend it with people you love? This all happened because of me. I don't know how to feel."

"Champagne, you can't keep blaming yourself—"

"Then who do I blame?" she yells at Marcy. "If I don't blame myself you tell me who is responsible for this shit? Because, it damn sure wasn't my mother and goddaughter. Yet they took the bullets."

"Crystal," Marcy says flatly. "Crystal alone is responsible for everything we going through right now. And, although we know that, it doesn't change the situation, or bring your people back. We in over our heads now, and we gotta swim or drown."

"My goddaughter just had a birthday," Champagne continues. "And now her life has been snuffed out. I swear on everything, I don't know what I'm going to do when I see Crystal's face again. I'm gonna fuck that pretty little face of hers all the way up. Believe that."

Since everyone seems to believe that we look an awful lot alike, I lay down in the seat so she doesn't see my face. I don't want to be target practice.

"This is why I want you to start thinking about yourself," Marcy says pointing at her. "You think I'm being selfish, but it's my responsibility to think that way. Do you know the definition of selfishness?"

"I don't care," Champagne responds.

"Well I do," Marcy says to her. "Selfish means to be concerned chiefly with one's own personal profit or pleasure. If something is wrong with that, I don't give a fuck. You, and you alone gotta worry about you. Because, trust me when I say, everybody else will care for themselves. I'm just saying."

"I'm broken right now," Champagne says dropping her head. "I'm so broken."

"Well then fix yourself up again," Marcy responds. "Do it for yourself. Please, Champagne, I need you tough and strong."

I thought tough and strong meant the same thing.

"I'm trying," Champagne whispers. "I swear to God I'm trying."

"Well try harder," Marcy says with an attitude hitting the steering wheel. "Fuck! Get mad out this mothafucka. It's time to fight. That's the only way you survive."

"You gonna always be this way, aren't you?" Champagne asks Marcy.

"I don't know what you talking about."

"Yes you do," Champagne says turning her body around in the passenger seat, to look at Marcy's face. "You think what you went through as a kid is common, don't you? Death and violence are as easy as breathing for you."

Marcy's body seems to stiffen. "I can't talk about other people's lives, and what's common for them, Champagne. I can only speak on mine."

"I'm sorry you saw that happen to your parents," Champagne says softly. "But, that was not normal."

"Well it was my normal," Marcy responds in an evil tone.

"And I respect that," Champagne continues, "but it wasn't normal."

Marcy turns around in the driver's seat, and drops her head. "They were all I had in the world. I wanted to be like my mother, and father when I was younger. I wanted the money, the cars and the clothes. They were like superstars to me. They had it all, Champagne. Friends, money, cars, and love. And, to think that it was all taken away from us, just because my father's side bitch got jealous, fucks my mind up. How the side bitch kill the family?" She hits her head with a closed fist. "She wasn't playing her position, and it hurts."

"I know it's wrong," Champagne says placing a hand on Marcy's thigh. "I can see how it would mess your mind up too, but what happened was not normal. Nobody burns a house down with a family inside of it. You feel bad because you ran out of that house and saved yourself, but your parents would've wanted you too. Who else was going to take care of your brother?"

"You don't know what you talking about," Marcy says in a low voice. "I was a punk. I ran because I was scared. I was supposed to die with them in that house. And, then we would've been together to this day. And, I wouldn't be alone."

"Marcy, you gonna have to learn how to love again, or this evil inside of you will kill you," Champagne says.

"Bitch, don't act like I'm the only one doing wrong in this car," Marcy responds. "You get money no matter what just like me. We both killed together, so we both are evil."

"Yes we do kill, but I still know how to love. You don't, Marcy."

"So you saying I don't love, Tiffany?" Marcy asks clenching her fist. "You saying I don't love my daughter?"

"I'm saying you didn't give birth to her," Champagne responds. "I'm saying you found her abandoned in that hallway, after we killed her family and you felt guilty. I'm saying you raised her as your own, and did the best you could to take care of her. And, I'm saying because you never had that maternal bond with her, you didn't know how to love her properly. I'm also saying that you are angry for Child Care Services taking her away from you, after everything you did for her, so you killed that girl back at the house the other day."

There is nothing, but silence in the car now. I feel like in any minute something is going to blow up. These two bitches are full of secrets. I'm sure Marcy is going to hit Champagne, instead Marcy's phone rings. With her eyes still on Champagne, she places the phone on speaker.

"Hello," Marcy says.

"So by now you see that I'm not playing," someone says into the phone.

I'm not sure, but I got a feeling it's Axe. A chill rolls through my body, and I suddenly feel very cold.

"Axe, why did you take my family away from me," Champagne cries into the speaker. "They had nothing to do with this shit. You took everyone from me."

"I didn't take everybody from you," he says. "But, I will. And, that goes for your family too, Marcy. I know about your daughter, who is being taken care of by that Asian family out Virginia. I will murder them all if my brother does not come back to me."

"But, we didn't do anything to you," Marcy says. "Crystal did."

"Bring her to me then," he says. "Let me question her properly, and I will call the dogs off of you."

"Give us some time," Marcy says.

"You have no more time. I suggest you move now, and hope I don't do anything else to show my vengeance. I want my brother, and I don't believe no story about no carjacking either. Bring him to me now."

He hangs up, and they don't say anything to each other for five minutes. I don't know what they're thinking, but one things for sure, I'm not taking that meeting with Axe as

Crystal. They will be short fucking with me. That's on everything.

When the phone rings again my heart feels like it stops. I beat it once with my fist, just to feel better.

"Hello," Marcy says. The phone is on speaker again.

"Hi, Marcy, it's me, Crystal."

Champagne and Marcy look at each other with anger.

"Crystal, things have changed between us forever," Marcy says. "And, you need to come home."

"What happened?" Crystal responds. "You sound like I did something to you."

"Where are you?" Champagne asks calmly, although the ripples in her forehead tell me she is beyond angry.

"Still in Philadelphia," Crystal says. "Why?"

"Because Axe murdered my family," Champagne says. "My mother and my goddaughter are both gone."

"And, he's threatening to harm mine next," Marcy says.

Crystal breaks into a cheap cry. I've heard better crying on episodes of 'You Are Not The Father' on the Maury Povich show. I'm not impressed at all.

"I'm sorry, ya'll," Crystal says. "I don't care what I have to do. I'm coming home to face Axe myself. Please forgive me. Please!"

# WILD WEDNESDAY DAY FIGHT

## Chapter Twenty-Three

The three of us walk through a tiny hallway of a New York City apartment building. After climbing some stairs, Champagne opens the door to apartment 344. Marcy and I walk inside, and Champagne locks the door. She throws her keys, and purse on a tiny brown couch over by the window.

I don't know who lives here, but the place is so small they can't be comfortable. There are a lot of pictures on the wall, and the heat is almost unbearable. I guess New Yorkers don't believe in air conditioning.

"Y'all can sit down," Champagne says dryly. "Did you want something to drink?" She asks looking at us.

I sit on a hard green metal chair, and Marcy sits on the sofa. It hurts my ass immediately, because of the stab wound, but I'm use to it by now.

"Is any alcohol in here?" I ask. "Like a fruity vodka or something?" I adjust the big shades on my face.

"I'll take whatever you got," Marcy says.

Feeling that I may be left out for being too specific I say, "I'll take whatever you got too. I just need a buzz."

Champagne walks to the refrigerator and comes back out with three Smirnoff vodka drinks. They are coconut flavored. She hands us one, and keeps the other for herself.

"Are you sure I'm supposed to be in here?" Marcy asks Champagne. "Because, you know she don't fuck with me like that. Never has and never will."

"You know is not even like that," Champagne responds.

"It's exactly like that," Marcy says sipping her drink. "She told me to my face, and me and her got into it before and everything. And, I don't feel like dealing with her right now."

I wonder what they're talking about. Before, we even came into the door; I felt the tension in the room. It's amazing how you can experience negative energy with the person not even being home. It feels like this sometimes when I go to my house. All the bad memories, and stuff make me uncomfortable. I feel uncomfortable here too.

"Just relax," Champagne says to Marcy sitting on the sofa. The couch is so small their knees knock together. "You know I had to come here to make sure she knows what happened to her sister. She's going to be devastated. My mother was the glue that kept this family together. And, now she's gone."

When the door opens a woman about five foot eleven enters the apartment. She's wearing a blue bus driver's uniform. Her hair is corn rowed to the back. The look on her face seems stressed, until she sees Champagne's face.

Champagne stands up and walks over to her.

"What are you doing here, Baby Girl?" The woman asks. "I thought you would be in DC finalizing things."

"I can't stay there," Champagne says. "You know I'm wanted." Champagne looks at the watch on her arm. "You home early."

"I got off work early so that I could drive down to DC to come see you." Bus Driver starts crying as she hugs Champagne. "I'm so sorry, Baby Girl. I know how much your mother meant to you. You speak to your uncle yet?"

"They say he's going off right now," Champagne says to her. "They say anybody who has a beef with him in the streets should not leave the house tonight. Aunt Wendy, it don't look good at all."

"Is it true what they said?" Wendy frowns rubbing Champagne's arms.

"What you talking about?" Champagne questions.

"Niggas are telling me that the bitch Marcy you run with may be involved in all of this," Wendy replies.

The hairs on the back of my neck rise. I heard when Marcy said that Wendy doesn't like her, but I didn't realize how deep the hatred went. I could hear the dislike in Wendy's voice when she said Marcy's name.

"Aunt Wendy, don't say that," Champagne replies. "This don't have shit to do with Marcy."

"Hello, Wendy," Marcy says sipping her vodka. "How was work?"

Wendy turns around on her heels and rushes toward Marcy. She clenches both of her fist, looks down at her, and says, "What the fuck are you doing in my house, bitch? You know I don't fuck with you like that."

Marcy takes another sip of her vodka, and Wendy snatches it out of her hand, and throws it down. The bottle rolls on the floor, and the drinks spills out onto the thin cream carpet.

Marcy jumps up, and stares Wendy into the eyes. Before this moment I didn't know Marcy was the same height as Wendy. Maybe she isn't. But, I can tell you one thing standing next to Wendy, Marcy looks just as tall.

"Wendy, I don't got no beef with you," Marcy says calmly. "And, I hate that you look at me the wrong way."

"I know exactly what kind of person you are," Wendy replies. "Since my niece has been involved with you, you have done nothing but bring her down. If she's not getting locked up, she's getting tied up with killers and murderers. Half of New York and Philadelphia don't fuck with you two no more. If it wasn't for how my name rings in the cities, my niece would be dead right now. So don't spit that stupid shit you saying to me. I know you too well."

"Wendy, Champagne is a grown woman," Marcy says to her. "If she don't want my company all she has to do is say the word, and I'll leave." Marcy looks at Champagne. "Is that how you feel, Champagne? Do you want me gone?"

"Aunt Wendy, I know you don't like Marcy," Champagne replies. "But, I think if you gave her a chance you would really like her. You know don't nobody make me do anything I don't want to do. And, that goes for Marcy too. I am my own woman. I'm my own bitch. Believe that, if you believe nothing else."

Wendy turns her head around to look at her niece. "I knew you since you were this tall," Wendy says raising her hand a little above the floor. "I changed your diaper, I sang to you when you were a little girl, and I know your heart. You not no killer, but this bitch is." She points at Marcy. "And, if you continue to roll with her you're going to pay for it with your life. You already have, Champagne. Don't you see everything that you've lost?"

"You got to let me live my life," Champagne says to Wendy. "That's all you can do."

You're right about that," Wendy says to her. "But, it doesn't mean that I have to allow this bitch," she continues pointing a stiff finger into Marcy's chest, "into my house."

I don't have to know Marcy long enough to tell you that Wendy putting a hand on her was a bad move. Marcy looks like she changed a different color…somewhere between red and dark burgundy.

Before I know it, I saw Marcy reach behind her back with her right hand, and grab her gun. It was too late to warn anybody else, because, just as soon as I saw it, Marcy was blowing Wendy's heart to the wall.

Wendy's body fell backwards into the TV, and then the floor. Wendy grips her chest, and then her hands drop to her sides. Her eyes roll to the back of her head, and her mouth hangs open. Blood crawls from under her back like a puddle of water. Wendy lets out one last sigh, and I know she died.

Champagne runs over to Wendy. She drops to her knees, and pulls her upper body toward her breasts. She does the same thing she did when her father died of the heroin overdose. She rocks her aunt's upper body in her arms as if she were a baby. Although Champagne's mouth is open, it takes a second before any sound comes out. But, when it does, it's a long hard cry.

I feel so bad for Champagne. She's experienced more death than any one person should handle in a week.

"Why did you do that?" Champagne cries looking up at Marcy. "Why would you take something else from me?"

"I was defending myself," Marcy responds.

Champagne stands up and approaches Marcy. She takes her right hand, and slaps Marcy across the face. A bloody handprint rests on Marcy's cheek, but Marcy seems unfazed.

"You're a fucking liar," Champagne screams pointing a finger in her face. "You are a liar if you are nothing else!"

Marcy doesn't move. They are so focused on one another that nobody sees that I am now next to the front door. I was able to wiggle myself all the way out of the line of fire. And, if Marcy touches that gun again, New York or not, I'm gone.

"Lift her shirt up," is all Marcy says to Champagne.

Champagne cries. "What?"

"I say look under her shirt," Marcy repeats.

Champagne turns her body around, and looks down at her aunt. From where I stand I look toward her shirt too. My mouth drops when I see the handle of a silver gun lying against Wendy's stomach. It's raised all the way up. The barrel is the only thing tucked into her uniform pants. It looks like she was about to pull it out, but didn't get a chance.

"She was about to kill me," Marcy says to Champagne. "Now if you want to fight me, I'm with that shit. But, I had to defend myself, or I was going to die. So what do you want to do? You want to blame me for this? Or do you want to put this behind us?"

Champagne doesn't respond. She's crying. She's crying really hard.

Marcy walks around her and toward me at the door. Marcy grabs the keys to the Benz off of the sofa. "Me and Crystal will be waiting downstairs in the car," she says referring to me. I don't bother to remind her of my name. "If you're coming with us you got 20 minutes to grieve, but not a minute more."

# Chapter Twenty-Four

We are in a cheap motel in New York, sitting in the dark. An open window gives up a little light. Marcy and Champagne have not said a word to each other since Marcy murdered her aunt.

There are two beds in the room. Two twin sized beds. Marcy is sitting on the bed closest to the window, looking out of it. She's been puffing cigarette after cigarette, and a huge cloud hovers over the top of her head.

Champagne and me are lying together on the other bed. She's in front of me weeping softly, and I'm behind her rubbing her hair. I guess you could say we were spooning. What an awful night.

As I look at Marcy's dark silhouette I'm confused. I don't get her. If you say you love your friend, how can you hurt her so badly? Where most people use violence as a last resort, it seems that violence is Marcy's first choice.

"Crystal, you probably think I'm evil for what I did back there don't you?" Marcy asks me.

"My name is Porsche," I tell her. It feels so good to put her in her place. "I appreciate if you call me by my name from here on out."

"My bad," Marcy responds turning around to look at me. "Like I was saying, Crystal, you probably think I'm some sort of monster don't you?" She looks back out the window.

I hate that bitch so much. Until this point in my life I never met a person that I had extreme hate for. Yes, my mother got on my nerves. And, yes I felt used by people like

Chris down the block from my house. But, nobody, and I do mean nobody, made me feel extreme rage before Marcy.

"Come on, Marcy," I say to her, "we all know it doesn't matter what I think. You are who you are I guess." I continue to stroke Champagne's hair.

"I'm serious," she says turning around from the window to look at me again. "I really want to know. Do you think I'm a monster? Do you think I'm evil?"

"I don't think you're a monster," I respond.

I think she smiles, but it's so dark I can barely see her face.

"I know you're a monster," I say to her. "Only monsters hurt their friends and family. But, I know you don't need me to tell you that. I'm just a little dirty girl from up the block."

She looks angry now. But, I've come to the point where I know that what ever is going to happen will happen. It doesn't pay to be afraid of every single thing that she does anymore. If I stay scared of everything, my blood pressure would go through the roof. I prefer to stand on my own two feet. Of course that may change tomorrow, if I'm still alive, but for right now that's how I feel.

"Bitch, you don't know shit about me," Marcy yells pointing her cigarette in my direction. "So you think you can hang around me for seven or eight days, and be able to draw conclusions? You don't even know 1% of what I can do or what I'm capable of. I held back since you've been around. But, more than anything you don't know what I've gone through, or how I feel about Champagne. She's one of my best friends, and I love her."

She may be right, but I don't understand why she would ask my opinion if she really didn't want to hear it. I don't say anything else to her. I just continue to rub Champagne's hair. Champagne is not crying as hard as she was before, so I hope that I'm offering peace.

"There comes a time when you have to push off," Marcy continues looking out of the window.

I think she's talking to me, but I can't be sure. I'm never sure.

Marcy drinks everything that is in the first gin bottle on the table, before moving to the next. "Remember that."

I get up off the bed, and drink the already mixed Long Island iced tea in my bottle. I drink this stuff so much now that I can tell when it's mixed freshly or manufactured like this drink. I down everything in my first bottle anyway, and move to my second.

Instead of going back over to the bed, I sit at the table in the room, and look at Marcy's silhouette again. I think about Brillo. I wonder if he's alive or dead. I wonder what he would say to Champagne and me if he were in our shoes right now. Would he kill Marcy? Or would he run? I wonder what kind of person he is. Is he a killer just like his brother Axe? Or, does he have a heart like me?

Champagne rolls out of the bed, and goes to the bathroom. She closes the door, and turns the water on. I can still hear her crying despite the running water, but I leave her alone. Everybody needs time alone, whether they know it or not.

About fifteen minutes later Champagne comes back out of the bathroom, and looks at me. "Walk me outside," she says to me. And, then she looks at Marcy. "Can I borrow a cigarette?"

Marcy shrugs. "Knock yourself out," Marcy responds to Champagne. "It's a free country."

Champagne walks toward Marcy, grabs the cigarette pack off the windowsill, and takes out two. She throws the pack back down, and it drops to the floor. She doesn't bother to pick it back up. She walks away.

"That was real classy," Marcy says picking up the cigarette pack and placing it back on the windowsill. "I'll be happy when you get your shit together. Because, the weak Champagne leaves nothing to be desired."

Champagne doesn't respond to her. She opens the front door, and I follow her outside. When the door closes behind her she looks at me.

"You smoke?" She asks holding out the extra cigarette.

I take it even though I don't smoke. I just like to be able to do something with my nervous hands. She places the cigarette between her pouty lips, and I do the same. She lights my cigarette, and then her own. She inhales, and then blows out a large puff of smoke. I imitate her, but choke hard. I hit my chest twice, and drop the cigarette on the ground, and step on it. Damn a cancer stick!

Champagne laughs at me, and shakes her head. Pointing at me with the lit cigarette she says, "You are funny."

The corner of my mouth hikes up. I feel stupid yet again. "I don't try to be," I admit. She's acting like I'm a clown.

"I know," Champagne tells me. "That's why I like you so much. With you what you see is what you get. It's refreshing," she continues pulling on her cigarette. "You should be proud of yourself."

"Proud of myself for what?" I inquire really wanting to know.

"You live in one of the most body conscious cities in the world," she says blowing out smoke. "But, somehow you managed to maintain some small semblance of yourself. Do you know how many people have lost themselves in DC? Hundreds of thousands. And, do you know why?"

I shake my head no. Besides, if I know nothing else I know that Champagne and Marcy love to hear themselves talk.

"Because they're too busy trying to live for everybody else," she continues. "You aren't like that though are you?"

"I don't know why I am the way I am," I tell her honestly. "I guess I'm just trying to figure it all out."

"We got to get away from her," Champagne says out of nowhere. "We gonna die if we don't."

My heart is thumping again. My heart is thumping hard. I feel like I'm on the verge of a heart attack. Because, if Champagne is saying that we had to get away from Marcy it means that Marcy's current personality is so far off from who she really is that we aren't safe. And, since she was already dangerous, I figure she must be Hitler now.

"Why you say that?" I asked.

"Because, I heard her on the phone earlier today," Champagne says. "It was when you used her fake ID to go to the liquor store and stock up. She thought I was asleep, but I wasn't. She was in the bathroom making some deal with Axe that doesn't include us. So, I don't trust her anymore. Not to mention the fact that she killed my favorite aunt."

I want to console her again, but every time I do she seems to cry harder.

"So when do we go?" I ask.

"Now," she says.

I lean into her. "Now?" I repeat. "We not going to wait for her to go to sleep or nothing?"

"We don't have time for all of that," she tells me. "Besides, Marcy never sleeps until everybody else around her do. So it's now or nothing. Are you scared or something?"

"If your best friend wasn't a serial killer, I probably wouldn't be scared," I tell her. "But, since that's not the case…"

She takes the cigarette out of her mouth, and smashes it on the ground. She grabs me by my wrist, and pulls me toward the car. She doesn't even give me a chance to get my mind right. She wants to leave Marcy, and she wants to leave Marcy now.

We make it to the Benz, and she reaches into her pocket for the keys. "Oh shit," she yells patting her pocket.

"Looking for these?" Marcy says standing behind us, dangling the keys in the air.

# THICK THURSDAY

# DAY NINE

# Chapter Twenty-Five

We're in Maryland now. Marcy is driving the car, and nobody has said a word to nobody, including me. Marcy may have been mad when we tried to leave her in New York, but she didn't show it. She's as cool as the breeze coming out of the air conditioner. So, if you ask me that makes her scarier than ever.

The last thing I heard, before me and Champagne tried to run and save ourselves, was that Crystal was going to meet us somewhere in Maryland. But, all morning both Marcy and Champagne have been trying to reach Crystal, and she still won't return calls.

"I need you to pull in that gas station up the street," Champagne says to Marcy. "I got to use the bathroom."

"I ain't stopping," Marcy replies turning the music up on the radio.

Champagne looks at Marcy, and gives her the evil eye. "Oh yes you are too," Champagne says with major attitude. "Now I said I have to go to the bathroom, and since this is my car you are going to stop." She turns the radio off.

"I ain't stopping," Marcy repeats driving down the street. "Now chill. You too hot right now."

Oh shit! Here they go. I already know things are about to get all the way out of control.

"Marcy, I'm not playing with you," Champagne says breathing heavily. "Stop this fucking car."

"And, I say I'm not doing it," Marcy says looking at her, and then the road. "I stopped thirty minutes ago, and went to the bathroom. Before I did that I made an announcement to nobody in particular, and nobody in particular but me got out and used the toilet. So either piss in your pants, or wait until we get to where we going."

"You want to fight me," Champagne says. "Don't you? Because, it seems like you're doing everything you can to piss me off."

"Champagne, you think too highly of yourself. I don't give a fuck about you or that ratchet bitch in the backseat. So slow your roll, and relax your mind, because I'm not stopping this car, until I want to. So please catch that."

"Oh yes you are stopping too," Champagne replies cracking her knuckles.

"Can we just stop fighting?" I ask them both. "Because, all of this is out of control now. You and her have been friends for way too long to be doing all of this."

"Bitch, shut your musty ass up," Marcy says to me. "You not even all my level. So don't wear the uniform when you not in my league."

"I don't need to be on your level," I say growing irritated with them treating me like a stepchild.

"Thank God," Marcy laughs at me. "Because I'm still trying to figure out what kind of bitch are you to take off a pair of $200 jeans, with over $1000 in the pocket, to dance at the bar in cotton draws for 15 bucks."

My nose burns. I'm so embarrassed.

"I took my draws off," I correct her. "I wasn't dancing in them."

"I'm glad you cleared that up, sweetie," Marcy continues laughing harder. "It don't matter what you did, because you still came up short in the long run," Marcy replies. "And then you got my fake ass friend over here plotting to leave me in New York. The funny thing is you all Team Champagne, and you don't even know what's going on. Champagne is working your ass over some kind of good, little girl. Pay attention. But, since you've never played in the major leagues before you can't see it," Marcy laughs. "You so green, you grassy."

I don't know what she's talking about. My heart is beating fast again, because I'm confused.

"Marcy…pull…this…car…over…now," Champagne demands. "That's my final warning."

"Well, you could've left your final—,"

Champagne hits Marcy so hard in the face, that she relocates her lips to the window for a minute. Spit splatters on the window, along with a few drops of blood.

Marcy whips the car over to a Laundromat parking lot, and she looks mad about it too. Both Champagne and Marcy get out of the car, and leave the doors open. I don't bother to open my door, besides from where I am I got the best seat in the house.

Marcy hits Champagne in the face so hard, Champagne lifts off her feet, and drops to her back. Marcy jumps on Champagne, and straddles her body. She grabs the front of Champagne's shirt, and hits her three more times in the face. Marcy then proceeds to get up, and kick her on the left side of her body five extra times.

"Get the fuck up," I scream to myself inside the safety of the car.

Marcy is beating her so badly I feel bad for watching.

Finally Champagne makes an attempt to stand up, but Marcy kicks her in her stomach, and Champagne falls face first back on the ground. Marcy rolls Champagne on her back and comes down on her stomach with an elbow. At this point I've seen enough.

I get out of the car, and grab Marcy's long hair from the back. I'm not a fighter, so I immediately feel like I don't know what I'm doing. But, since I'm involved now I have to see this thing through.

Marcy manages to get every last piece of her hair out of my grasp, and bust me in the face with one of those sleepers she gave Champagne. Thanks to this blow I have a fat lip to match my fat eye.

I take off running in the opposite direction, but Marcy catches me a few feet out, and jumps on my back. I go chin first on the ground, and bite my tongue. I taste my own salty blood. I roll over, and start kicking and hitting her everywhere I can. But, as I get a glimpse of Marcy's face I see that it is flawless. Which, means we haven't landed blow one on this bitch.

I pray for help, when I see Champagne running up to us from behind. Champagne hits Marcy in the back of the head with a closed fist. Marcy gets up off of me, and beats Champagne like a percussion instrument in band class. I don't understand why Marcy is so strong. How can somebody so pretty, be so Mike Tyson like?

When I see Marcy move for the gun in the small of her back, I know now that things have gone too far. I get up off the ground, and grab Marcy from the back with an arm to the throat. I finally dig my nails into the flesh of her nose with my other hand and pull back. When she screams, and drops the gun, I know that I finally got a good one in. She turns around and directs her hate toward me. She looks madder than ever now.

I'm about to kick the gun toward Champagne when Marcy gets a hold of the gun again. Breathing heavily she cocks the gun and says, "Don't nobody move." I laugh when I see I've scratched her pretty little face. "Throw them in the air!"

We both put our hands up.

"Now walk over to the car," Marcy demands.

We turn around and walk toward the car with our hands still in the air.

"Sit on the hood," Marcy tells us.

We both sit on the warm hood of the Mercedes Benz.

"I got a mind to shoot both of you bitches in the throat," Marcy says to us. "So what you got to do is tell me why I shouldn't."

"Marcy, do whatever the fuck you want," Champagne replies. "I'm just saying."

Marcy laughs. "You don't mean that shit," she replies. "You're just mad because I got the best of you."

"You have a gun on us in broad daylight," Champagne says. "So either shoot us or get the fuck up out my face." Champagne spits out blood to her right. "I can't even count the number of times you've pointed a gun in my face. And, guess what, I'm still here. So either you missing or not shooting."

"You really feeling yourself right now aren't you?" Marcy asks.

"You're just mad because you're holding a gun at me, and I could care less. I'm done being afraid of what you may say or do to me," Champagne says to Marcy. "My aunt was right about you. You ain't nothing but a sheisty ass bitch."

"I'm sheisty," Marcy says pointing the gun at herself.

"Yes you are sheisty," Champagne says placing her hands on her hips.

"How about you tell your friend about the deal we made with Axe," Marcy laughs.

"I don't know what you talking about," Champagne responds.

"Oh sure you do, my little, buddy-friend," Marcy replies.

"Are we going to meet Crystal or what?" Champagne says. I think she's trying to skip the subject.

"Not until you tell your friend about the price placed on her head," Marcy continues. "Don't cheat me out of the look on her face. The shit is going to be priceless."

"I'm walking back to the car," Champagne says.

"Okay, well I'll tell her myself," Marcy says.

Champagne stops walking, and turns around to look at us. I wonder what’s going on now.

"Porsche," Marcy says finally calling me by my name, "your little lover over there, and I spoke to Axe on the phone earlier today. And, in exchange for you, as the fake Crystal of course, we will be earning $20,000 if we turn you in. But, your boo over there decided to leave me in New York and get the money herself. She was being greedy."

My feelings are hurt.

"That's not true," Champagne says to me. "If it were true why would we be trying to meet up with the real Crystal?"

"Because, Axe says he'll give us $20,000 more for his brother," Marcy laughs. "He said he just has to know what happened to his family. We need Crystal for that small piece of the puzzle. Now isn't that right Champagne?"

I don’t know what to believe.

I don’t know who to believe.

I’m so confused.

# FALL OUT FRIENDS FRIDAY

# DAY TEN

# Chapter Twenty-Six

We are sitting in a car at Arundel Mills Mall waiting on Crystal's call again. We all got busted faces.

Earlier we went out to eat, and I didn't say anything to either of them. Both of them were trying to be extra nice to me. And, it seems that the physical situation we got into yesterday brought them closer together.

*"Porsche, do you want some more Long Island,"* Champagne asked earlier today at the restaurant. *"It's my treat."*

*"Porsche, you want a new shirt from the mall?"* Marcy asked me. *"I got a hook up at one of the stores."*

They are doing everything in their power to appease me, and that makes me more nervous. If they are trying to keep me, it means they need me. And, if they need me, it means they are trying to put the blame on me.

"Did she say she would meet us over here by the movies?" Champagne asks Marcy from behind the steering wheel. "Or the bookstore?"

"You were on the call just like me," Marcy snaps. "I guess we just got to wait again until she comes."

"She's not coming," I say looking out the window at the parked cars. "All of us know it."

They turn around and look at me. I guess it's strange that I made that statement the first thing I chose to say all day.

"And, why do you think that?" Marcy asks me. "She seemed real sorry about what happened to Champagne's family earlier when I spoke to her on the phone."

"She's not coming," I repeat choosing to be as mysterious as they normally are. The look on their faces is priceless to me.

"Well, she doesn't have a choice," Champagne says. "After everything she's done to me, she needs to be here."

"She doesn't give a fuck," I say.

"You don't know what you're talking about," Champagne responds. "I've been knowing that girl all of my life."

"Well, I feel sorry for you," I say. "I guess you have to pick your friends better."

"She's right," Marcy says to Champagne. "Crystal isn't coming. But, I think I have an idea. I don't know why I didn't think of this before."

"What is it?" Champagne asks.

"What does Crystal care about no matter what?" Marcy asks.

Champagne shrugs her shoulders. "What is the answer, because to tell you the truth I have no idea."

Marcy points at her and says, "That's because you're not using your head. Take some time to think about what Crystal does religiously every week."

"This is getting weak," Champagne responds.

"Just do it," Marcy yells. "What does she do religiously each week?"

I'm on pins and needles. I called myself being mysterious by giving them five and six word responses earlier, but they quickly remind me of who the true Queens of Mystery really are.

"I honestly don't know," Champagne replies looking at Marcy.

"Well luckily for you, I do," Marcy says.

We are sitting in front of a beautiful building in Washington DC. It looks like a church, but its kind of different.

"What's this?" I ask Marcy looking out of the window.

"A mosque," Marcy says loading her gun.

"So why are we here?" I ask watching her.

I'm shaking again. And, whenever I shake it means something bad is going to happen.

"We are here because every Friday no matter what," Champagne says, "Crystal comes here." Champagne shakes her head as if she finally gets it. "It's called Jumu'ah…its their prayer."

"But why?" I ask.

"Because she's Muslim," Marcy says wresting the gun in her lap.

"But, how can she be Muslim?" I ask. "Aren't they strict in terms of religion? I mean, doesn't she have premarital sex, and all kinds of stuff like that? "

"Every religion has sinners," Marcy replies looking back at me. "The sooner the world realizes it, the sooner things will change for the better."

Champagne shakes her head. "I don't know why I didn't think of this before. We could of come here the day Beeper raped Porsche."

My heart drops. Although, I know I didn't forget the rape, I tried to put it out of my mind by drinking. And now I'm being reminded. *Thanks for nothing, Champagne.* I think.

"If I'm not mistaken that was also Friday," Champagne continues looking at Marcy.

"Please don't bring my brothers name up again," Marcy says with an attitude. "You know he has Down syndrome."

I sigh and shake my head. She makes me so mad excusing him for what he did, just because he's sick.

"That's not what I'm saying," Champagne says. "Had we come here last Friday my family would be alive today." She looks at Marcy, and then at me. "That's what I'm saying. We could've came to this church, pulled her out, and dealt with this shit a long time ago."

"Damn," is all I can say.

Champagne looks down at the gun in Marcy's lap. "Marcy, I know that you're crazy, and I know you're thorough, but if you go up in there with some bullshit I'm calling the police. You already killed a kid. I'm not trying to go to jail, because you're shooting up this holy temple."

Marcy laughs. "Calm down," she replies. "Nobody is going in, we are waiting for her to come out. And, I'm not leaving this building until she does."

An hour later I spot Crystal first. Marcy and Champagne don't see her yet, because they are too busy arguing again. I'm starting to realize that they aren't themselves without fussing and fighting with each other all day.

But, there she is, the girl…the girl of the hour. The one we've all been waiting for. She's standing on the steps talking to two women. From here I can tell that her brown bob is much shinier and prettier than mine. The long sleeve cream shirt she has on, and the black slacks make her look professional. Not like the freak-whore-slut that she is.

I know that in this moment I have the power to let her walk away. Her life right now is in my hands. If I say nothing there is a chance that Marcy and Champagne will never see her again. But, I know I can't do that. I'm in love with the idea of a person I've never met before. I want to know if Brillo is alive or dead, and I feel it's my responsibility to help him.

"There she is," I say to them.

They still don't hear me, because they're too busy arguing with one another.

When I see her approaching a car in a louder voice I say, "She's getting away."

"What you say, Crystal?" Marcy says on her bullshit again.

"The name is Porsche," I say. I point ahead of us. "And the real Crystal is getting away. Open your eyes and they might work."

"Oh shit," Marcy says throwing the car into drive. "We almost missed her ass."

I sit back in the seat and smile. I don't know why I'm smiling. Maybe it's because I'm looking forward to Crystal getting exactly what she deserves. Maybe it's because I'm looking forward to knowing Brillo's status. Or, maybe it's because I have more bad girl in me then I realized.

Who knows?

But, I guess I will find out.

# Chapter Twenty-Seven

I can't believe I'm hanging out with two killers in a public mall. But, it's not like we are shopping. No, that's not the case at all. We are here, because Princess Crystal felt it was necessary to shop while her friend's lives were in danger.

Champagne and Marcy are walking side by side. I'm behind them, and we are all several feet behind Crystal. We don't want her to see us yet.

"I can't believe this dirty bitch," Champagne says. "She's shopping."

"Believe it," Marcy whispers. I can see the bulge of the gun behind her shirt every time she moves. "This is the person you wanted to protect. So get a good look at her ass. Because, it's obvious she's giving it for you to kiss."

I'm looking at Crystal too. She's much thinner than me. But, her butt pokes out her jeans just like Marcy and Champagne's. My mind can only imagine all the nasty things she's done to Brillo with her nasty ass.

"Why would she do us like this?" Champagne asks as we get out of the way of an elderly couple.

"Because she's selfish," Marcy says. "She understands that at the end of the day, you gotta do what you can for yourself. And, you got to let other people sort the shit out. In some ways I admire her."

"Yeah, but in this case the other people are her friends," Champagne says to her. "The bitches who have had her back through thick and thin."

As they continue to run their mouths I think about what Axe is going to do to Crystal when he finally gets his hands on her. If he put bullets in Champagne's family, he'll probably get all-fancy and cut her head off. Maybe, she deserves it.

When Crystal walks into a high-end fashion store we sit on a bench some feet away from the entrance. We have newspapers in our hands to cover our faces, in case she comes out. The nerve of this bitch. I hate her so much I can't think of anything else right now.

When she finally comes out, she's carrying two bags in her hands. Two big bags at that.

"Ain't that some shit," Champagne says shaking her head. We all stand up, and leave the newspapers. "We running for our lives, and she out here shopping until she drops."

"It's cool though," Marcy replies. "Because, we almost to the finish line now. And, sooner or later, we gonna put this shit behind us."

"I hope so," Champagne says. "I say we go to Mexico after this shit. I need a vacation."

"I'm with that," Marcy responds. "But it ain't about hoping so," Marcy says. "It's about knowing so. By this time next week we will be on one of them chartered planes on an island in Cancun."

When Marcy turns away, Champagne frowns at her. I know Champagne still has resentment about what happened to her aunt. What I don't know is how it's going to play out yet.

When Crystal goes into another store, we stand a few feet back by some merry go-rounds.

"She's really doing the damn thing," Champagne says to Marcy. "I hate this bitch so much right now."

"You truly are preaching to the choir," Marcy replies.

Twenty minutes later Crystal is outside of the store with two more bags. She's holding so many bags now; it's hard for her to walk straight. She turns into the women's restroom.

"I can't believe the luck I'm having right now," Marcy says to Champagne. "I mean did she really just walk into the bathroom?"

"She sure did," Champagne says shaking her head slowly. "What a stupid ass bitch."

"Let's go get her," Marcy says.

We all creep towards the ladies bathroom. We look left and right before pushing inside. Once we are inside we don't see Crystal. Marcy walks out ahead of us and looks under all the stalls. From where I'm standing now I can finally see Crystal's feet.

Marcy walks softly toward us and whispers, "she's the only one here."

"Perfect," Champagne whispers also.

We all walk into a bathroom stall and close the doors. I guess we're waiting to make our move.

When a phone rings in the bathroom with a Frank Ocean song, I shiver. I know they're not stupid enough to leave their phones on at a time like this.

"Hi, daddy," Crystal says.

Oh snap! It's Crystal's phone.

"I'm sorry I haven't been answering my phone lately," Crystal continues, "I have a lot going on right now. But, I'll come visit the moment I can."

There is a moment of weird silence.

"Yes, daddy," Crystal says in a frustrated tone, "I went to service today."

She flushes the toilet. At least I think she flushes the toilet. I can't see what she's doing from here.

"Okay, daddy," Crystal says, "I have to go. I'll call you again when I can. I love you too, daddy. Very much. "

When I hear her door open I open mine also. The funny thing is Marcy and Champagne our already by the sinks. Waiting.

The color looks like it drains from Crystal's face when she sees Marcy and Champagne. And, then she gives the performance of a lifetime.

"Oh my, God," Crystal says running up to Marcy and Champagne with two arms full of shopping bags. "I was just about to call ya'll."

Marcy pushes Crystal back and looks at the bags in her hand. "You sure about that, Crystal?" Marcy replies. "Because from here it looks like the only thing you're doing is shopping."

"Wait…who beat ya'll's faces like that?" Crystal asks them.

"Shut the fuck up," Marcy says. "We asking questions not you."

"Gee, Crystal," Champagne says eying the bags also. "I want to be like you when I grow up."

"I know how this looks," Crystal says to them. "But, you have to hear me out. I haven't been home to wash my clothes, so I didn't have anything clean. I don't know where Axe is these days. I needed to come to the mall to buy something before I met up with y'all later. You know I love both of you, so don't act like that."

"I got to tell you, Crystal," Marcy says shaking her head, "from here it doesn't look like you care about nobody but yourself."

"You didn't even say anything about my family," Champagne says to her.

"Hold up," Crystal says throwing down her bags. "I know ya'll not gonna sit here and front like I don't love ya'll. Especially after everything we've been through together."

"I'm just telling you how it looks," Marcy says firmly. "You don't answer our phone calls. And, when we try to meet up with you, you give us the shaft. You not being an official bitch right now. You being something like a snake."

"I'm a snake," Crystal says pointing to herself. "Don't even act like I haven't rode with ya'll from day one. I have been missing in action, but it's not because I didn't love ya'll."

"So prove it," Marcy replies. "If you love us, give us proof."

"You coming with us to meet Axe," Champagne says. "Right now."

"But first we have to know where Brillo is," Marcy says.

"Please believe I don't have no problems with seeing Axe," Crystal says smacking her tongue, "especially after what that nigga did to my friend, and her family," she says looking at Champagne. "Axe got me all the way fucked up, and I'm going to tell him to his face too."

"Where is Brillo?" I ask Crystal.

Everyone looks at me like I'm the shit that won't go down the toilet.

"I'll tell ya'll all that later," Crystal says. "Right now I want to see Axe."

"Well there it is," Marcy announces. "Let me place this call, and tell him that we are on our way."

"Let's do it then," Crystal responds picking up her bags.

At this moment I know what Champagne and Marcy don't. And, that is that this bitch is going to run. No sooner than Marcy places her finger on the first digit, is Crystal out the door. Champagne and Marcy take off after her. I don't follow. Not yet anyway.

The moment I open the door I see Crystal, Marcy and Champagne talking to a mall officer. I slowly ease out of the bathroom, and away from them, but still in earshot.

"What's going on?" The black female officer says to the three of them. "Is everything okay here? Or, do we got a problem?"

# Chapter Twenty-Eight

I'm looking at the black female officer who in my opinion is doing too much for her job right now.

"Ma'am, I don't know these people okay?" Crystal says holding her bags. "I was rushing out so I can get to my meeting, and they happened to be rushing out too. Now unless you have something else to say to me, I'm gone." Crystal walks off without giving the officer a chance to dispute.

But, when Marcy and Champagne try to do the same thing the officer says, "Not so fast, I have to ask you two a few more questions."

"I got to go," Marcy says acting anxiously.

When I follow Marcy's eyes I can see she's watching Crystal get away.

"Listen, you not going anywhere until I say so," the officer continues. She radios something on her dispatch thingy and demand that they wait.

I back further away from them, and take the exit outside. When I'm not in view, I run as fast as I can. I should probably keep running home, but I don't. Instead, I go around the building, and walk up to a car. I do what I came to do, and patiently wait.

"Going somewhere?" I ask Crystal when I finally see her face.

"What do you want with me?" She says activating her alarm to throw the bags into the trunk. "Don't let them get you in our business." She slams the trunk closed. "We fight like this all the time, and we always get back together."

"I asked if you were going somewhere," I repeat with my hands on my hips.

"Look, Fake Crystal, either back up off of me or I'm gonna…,"

"You gonna do what, bitch," I say stepping closer to her.

I don't know where the fire came from. I guess it was an accumulation of everything I've gone through since I was forced to take over her life. For real I hadn't planned on coming at her like this, but she left me no other choice.

My plan was to ask about her family, and background. After the way my mother reacted when I asked her about other family members, it got me thinking that she may be hiding something. Maybe Crystal was a long lost cousin, for real I don't know.

"What did they tell you about me?" Crystal asks me in a softer voice.

"Not a lot of nice things," I respond leaning on her car. My ass hurts a little still, but I take it. "If you want to know the truth."

"What did they say exactly," she continues. "About me?"

"Besides the fact that you won't tell anybody where Brillo is, since you were the last person with him?" I say.

"Yes," she laughs. "Besides all of that."

"That's all they had to tell me," I say trying to act like she doesn't really matter. "Because, I didn't inquire about anything else. It's not like I'm a fan or nothing."

She laughs at me. "Ask me," she says sarcastically. "How about you ask me what they told me about you."

My heart is beating fast. Whenever this happens, it means I'm in for a whammy. Or, an embarrassing moment. The smile on her face is too concrete. It's like she knows something I don't. I can't stand when that happens.

"If you got something you want to tell me, just say it," I respond folding my arms over my chest.

"Well, for starters when Champagne first pulled up on you, she said your pussy stank raw," she starts. "So she had to take you to the hotel, and get you cleaned up. Because, to play a real bitch like me, you had to look and smell the part. So they gave you a pair of my True Religion jeans, and one of my Polo shirts. You were even able to rock my snakeskin *Michael Kors* sneaks," she looks down at my feet, "which you're currently rocking right now.

"Let me see," Crystal continues giving me more than I want to hear. "Oh yes, they also told me that you let White Daddy piss in your face, something he has been trying to get me to do for years, but I had a little too much respect for myself to be used in such a way. They did too, which is why they got you to do it.

"Oh, and they told me that you were playing with your pussy while Champagne was fucking a nigga from the back." She smirks. "Now, like I was saying, don't get it twisted, bitch, you could never be me. We fuss and we fight, but we ride with each other, always."

"I don't believe it," I say.

"You should, because this little thing that I have going on with my friends, shall pass. Just like the other problems that we have do."

I'm beyond embarrassed. My head hangs low.

"Hold your head up high," she tells me. "After all, you got to portray a real bitch, you should be proud of yourself."

It's mighty funny that Champagne and Marcy acted like they barely spoke to her, but the few times that they did, they managed to kick all of my business. And, who was running their mouth? Was it Marcy or Champagne? I guess it doesn't make a difference, but it would hurt more if it were Champagne.

"Now can you please be removed from my car," she says. "I got things to do."

I stand up, and walk away from her car. She's about to try and get away until I remember I flattened all of her tires. Just as I remember that, Champagne and Marcy approach me from behind.

"Good looking out, Porsche," Marcy says. I guess she remembers my name with the real Crystal present. "You stopped her." She looks at the tires.

Marcy and Champagne rush to the driver's side door and snatch Crystal out.

"You not getting away this time," Marcy says. "Take us to Brillo, and I don't give a fuck if he's dead or alive."

"Or if we got to dig him up," Champagne adds. "I got to see this nigga's face."

We pull up at a run down motel. I'm not just talking about a dirty motel. I'm talking about the kind of motel that is reserved for shitting, prostitutes and murders.

Marcy parks the car, and we all get out. Marcy grabs Crystal's forearm and says, "Which room is it?"

"Room 122," Crystal says with an attitude.

We walk around the back of the motel. And Marcy says to Crystal, "Where is your room key?"

Crystal digs into her pants pocket. "It's right here," she replies rolling her eyes.

Champagne snatches the key out of her hand, and opens the door. The moment she does we hear soft moaning. Like someone is in serious pain.

There are two twin beds inside of the room, and the one furthest from the door has someone lying on it.

"Oh my God," Champagne says. "Please tell me that's not Brillo," she says to Crystal.

Crystal doesn't say anything.

"Is it Brillo or not?" Champagne yells at her.

"You told me not to say anything," Crystal says with an attitude. "So do you really want to know or not?"

We all pile inside of the room. The door makes a loud sound when it slams behind us, and causes me to jump. We all walk toward the bed, but Marcy and Champagne are blocking me. I can't see his face. I need to see his face.

"Brillo," Champagne says softly, "are you okay?"

He's moaning like he's in a lot of pain. I wish everybody moves. I want to see him.

"Brillo, are you okay?" Champagne repeats.

"Get me to a hospital," he finally says. "Or I'm going to die."

"Crystal, I know we killed before," Marcy says in a shaken voice. "But, what would possess you to do this to Axe's brother? When you know the type of nigga he is?"

"The nigga cheated," Crystal responds sitting on the edge of the other bed. "So I dealt with him appropriately."

"What did you do?" Champagne asks.

"Since he likes to cheat, I cut off the hand that offended me."

# FALL OUT FRIENDS FRIDAY
# DAY TEN
# Chapter Twenty-Nine

Poor Brillo. I can't believe that bitch Crystal got mad at him, and cut off his hand. Who does that kind of vicious shit anyway?

Sighs. Well, at least they accepted my idea to move him to a cleaner hotel. They said yes to me, after a rat jumped on his arm, and threatened to chew his bloody stump off. Although I begged and pleaded with them for mercy, and to get him professional help, they still won't take him to the hospital. Brillo lost a lot of blood, and his skin looks ash grey, even though his pictures say he should be brown...like dripping honey.

We are in a two-room suite hotel, and I'm standing in the doorway looking at his face while he's lying in one of the full beds. He's asleep. Marcy and them are in the living room drinking their heads off, and suddenly I don't want anything. I feel sorry for Brillo, and I wish I could do more. Unfortunately, we're both slaves to the Drunk & Hot Girls' evil schemes.

Brillo coughs, rolls over and looks at me. I'm about to walk out of the room until in a weak voice he says, "Can you take me to the doctors?"

I walk deeper into the room, and sit on the full bed next to his. I comb my bushy bob with my fingers, and sigh.

"They won't let me," I say in a low voice. I look behind me to be sure they aren't coming. "I'll keep trying though." I look at his hand. "How do you feel? In much pain?"

His eyes lower. "I'm not doing too good," he responds. "It doesn't hurt as much as it did earlier. That scares me though. If I'm not in pain, it means the damage is probably worse."

He turns his head and looks out of the window. The sky is dark outside.

"Maybe I can get them to give you some more medicine," I say with wide eyes.

"You look like her," Brillo says to me. His voice is filled with hate.

"I know," I respond hating our resemblance. "But, I'm nothing like her. I would have never done this to you."

He turns back around and looks at me. "Prove it," Brillo says. "If you are nothing like them, help me get out of here." He looks at the open door and lowers his voice. "Or tell my brother where I am, so that he can come get me. If you not like them, doing that will make me believe you. If not, everything else you say is all talk."

"You are going home," I tell him, although I'm not sure if it's true or not. "It's just a matter of you getting better first."

"What you mean?" His forehead wrinkles a bit.

"They told me you are going home, but they don't want you to go back like this," I say. "They think Axe will be angry if he sees your hand cut off." I look at the bloody stump.

"So what they think, I'm going to grow another hand?" He yells at me. "Whether they take me back today or tomorrow, he still gonna be mad when he sees me like this."

I'm shaking. Brillo's mad at me, just because I know them. "Please, don't yell," I say. "They are holding me against my will too."

"You look pretty free to me," he says looking back out of the window.

"Do you know why she did that to your hand?" I ask trying to skip the subject.

"Crystal is crazy," he coughs again. "She doesn't understand that what she did to me, could kill me. She thinks this shit is a joke, but I don't. If I make it out of this alive I will get my hand on that bitch."

"I don't think she thinks its funny," I respond. "I think she's really scared."

"The longer she keeps me, the bigger the chance that I might die," he says in a low voice. "If she thought it was serious I wouldn't be here."

"That won't happen," I respond. "The thing you said about you dying."

"How you know?" He asks. His eyebrows rise. I can tell that he wants me to offer him hope.

"Because, I won't let you die," I promise him. "I won't let them kill you."

"Porsche," Champagne says calling me from the doorway.

I jump up off of the bed, and turn around. "What?" I yell totally annoyed.

Champagne frowns. I guess she doesn't like me speaking to her in that tone of voice. "Come here," she looks at Brillo. "I'll tell you what I want once you're out here." She walks away from the door, and it looks like she has an attitude.

I don't follow her right away. Instead, I walk over to Brillo. I place my hand on his shoulder. "I don't know how, but I will do everything I can to protect you," I say to him. "I need you to believe in me, even though you don't know me."

"I don't know why, Porsche," he coughs, "but for some reason, I do believe you. I just hope it doesn't prove to be a mistake."

I smile, and walk out of the room. The moment I step into the other part of the suite, Marcy is standing in my face. Her hair is pulled back into a tight ponytail, and she's smirking at me.

"What were ya'll in there talking about?" Marcy asks me dusting invisible particles off of her red sweatshirt.

I look behind her at her crew. Champagne and Crystal look like they are also waiting on my answer.

"I was just making sure he's okay," I say trying to sound tough. "Why, what's up out here?"

The are all silent. I hate that shit. Just say something already.

"We were just talking about Touching Todd," Marcy finally says to me. She walks over to the table, and pours something in a cup.

"What about him?" I ask. I hate talking about my uncle, especially after the reputation he built around the neighborhood.

"We were wondering about him," Marcy continues handing me a drink in a red cup.

"Marcy, just come out with it," I respond taking it from her hand. I take my first sip. It's my favorite...Long Island Ice Tea. "I don't know why you're beating around the bush. It’s not like you."

"Yeah, Marcy," Champagne continues, "Just tell her what you want already."

"We need you to get Todd here," Marcy says smoothing her hands down her thighs.

She walks back over to the table, and makes another cup of the same thing. She hands it to Crystal. It's only then that I remember that Long Island Ice tea was originally Crystal’s favorite drink, and that I just borrowed it.

"I don't talk to my uncle like that anymore," I respond putting my drink on the table. I walk over to the small black refrigerator on the floor, and grab a beer instead.

"Well we need you to take one for the team," Marcy replies folding her arms over her chest. "As much as we hate to admit it, he's our only option.

"Even if I wanted to reach out to him," I start, "which I don't," I continue taking a sip of beer, "what's my motivation?"

"We are trying to save Brillo's life," Crystal says. "And, since it's obvious that you want to protect him, we figured you'd be willing to do whatever you could to help him survive. I mean, you do like him don't you?"

My heart is beating fast. What did I do to put them on to the way I feel about Brillo? I drink the rest of my beer, and sit on the sofa in the room.

"How will my uncle save his life?" I squeeze the beer can in my hands to stay busy.

"Wasn't he a doctor?" Marcy asks with an attitude.

"Yes, but he's a gynecologist," I respond looking at their faces.

"Sweetie, gynecology was the practice he chose," Marcy says, "But, all doctors learn the basics. He knows how to save a life...trust me. We just got to get him here."

"That is, if you want Brillo to survive," Crystal says shooting eye daggers in my direction. I guess she doesn't like me cozying up to her man. But, it's too late for that now.

I hate Crystal so much. To tell you the truth I hate everybody in here, except Brillo and Champagne. Champagne has been going out of her way to apologize for what Crystal said to me outside of the mall. She assured me that it wasn't her who kicked my business to Crystal on the phone, but Marcy. And, I believe her.

"Why did you do it?" I ask Crystal. "Why did you cut his hand off?"

Crystal sighs. "I told you already," she shakes her head. "Because, I thought he was cheating." She sits on the floor, and pulls her knees to her chest. She takes a sip of her drink.

"You thought he was cheating with Dixon?"

Crystal nods.

"What gave you that impression?" I ask.

Crystal sighs again. "I was at the doctor's getting a pregnancy test one day," Crystal starts. "I fuck for money, but Brillo is the only nigga I fuck raw. So, when I missed my period, I thought I was pregnant. Anyway, I was in the doctor's office waiting on the pregnancy test results. When Dixon walks in with some dude with a scruffy beard, and brown glasses."

"Brown Glasses," I say remembering the dude that Marcy killed at Dixon's house.

"Yes, he was wearing brown glasses," she says sarcastically. "That's what I said."

"Go 'head," I say rolling my eyes. Nobody, but me knew I referred to him as Brown Glasses.

"Well, Dixon comes in and sits directly across from me with this dude. Dixon is crying her eyes out, and I hear her say that she is HIV positive. And, that she got the shit from Brillo. I thought my heart stopped," Crystal shakes her head. "This chick said Brillo came to see her yesterday, after Brillo came from the detail shop. I know he was at the detail shop that day, because he called me, and I believed her. I mean how else would she know that unless she was with him?"

"She was stalking him," I say. "She knew everything he did."

"I know that now, but I didn't know that then," Crystal responds rolling her eyes at me. "It all makes sense now, because Dixon started kicking a lot of other shit too. About places she could only know he's been if he told her. So, I asked Brillo about her over the phone. He said he knew the chick, and that she was cool with him. I think Brillo called her his play sister or something. He said, he would never go there with her, but I didn't believe him. He never told me about this bitch before. I never met his brother Axe, and I saw his sister Nita once at a party. It's like he was trying to hide something or me. It was like he was ashamed of me. So, in my mind he did fuck her."

"He didn't cheat with her," I say. "He was telling the truth. She was a virgin."

"Will you let me finish, damn?" Crystal yells at me. "Anyway, I was in my house when I asked him about her over the phone. I told him I wanted to pick him up to talk about a few things. But, Marcy and Champagne came over my house, because we had a job in Philadelphia. Before leaving the apartment I grabbed a knife to stab him later, and we all dipped out."

I'm thinking that the job they had to do in Philly was with White Daddy, but I can't be sure.

"The three of us went to pick Brillo up, and we grabbed something to eat. I couldn't really talk to him about it with Marcy and them around, so I dropped them off back at my apartment. When they were gone, Brillo was on the phone with his brother Axe at the time, who was in Jamaica. I remember wanting to bust him in his face. I wanted to talk."

"When he got off of the phone, I pulled on the side of the road, and asked him again was he fucking Dixon or not. He said no, and I didn't believe him. I took the knife out, and was about to stab him, but I loved him too much. So, I started jabbing myself in the leg instead. He was screaming and asking me what was going on. I didn't want him touching me, so I left out of the car, and ran into the middle of the street. I had blood all over me, and somebody from my neighborhood saw me. I guess that's how the rumor got started that I was shot, or dead.

"When I got back in the car Brillo looked really sad. Kept asking me what can he do to convince me that he loves me, and would never hurt me. Said he would do anything."

My feelings are hurt when I hear how much Brillo loves her. I feel overprotective of Brillo. Like he really belongs to me.

"I invited Brillo to the motel ya'll came too," Crystal continues. "And put three of Marcy's sleeping pills into his favorite beer. While he was sleep, I cut his hand off. I felt sorry about it after I did it, but it was much too late. The damage had already been done. And, that's what happened." She throws her hands up in the air. "I was going to kill him, but he begged me to verify if Dixon was HIV positive or not before I killed him. He said she was a liar, and that you couldn't believe anything she said, but that she was a sweet person. Just confused. When I found out she was HIV negative, I spared his life. I guess that's how we all ended up here."

"He's alive for now," Marcy responds. "Because, he's losing a lot of blood. Without your uncle he will die. You got to get him here, Porsche."

"Since, you know the story, now will you help him?" Crystal asks me.

# STABLE SATURDAY

# DAY ELEVEN

# Chapter Thirty

My uncle is in the room with Brillo. Everybody else is gone. I guess they wanted a mini-vacation. It probably has been tough on them these last few days, considering all of the people they killed. Poor little killers.

I'm nervous about Brillo's condition. When, my uncle first got here he said Brillo looked pretty bad. And, that if they waited one moment longer to call him, Brillo could've been dead. Needless, to say I'm sitting on edge.

After ten more minutes, my uncle Todd comes out of the room. His white button down shirt is covered in blood. He's wiping his hands with a bloody white towel, and he's breathing hard.

"That girl should be locked under the ground for what she did to that boy," Todd says to me, as if he has a clean criminal record himself. "I don't even know how he made it for as long as he did. He's fighting for something. It may be revenge."

"Is he okay?" I ask trying to peep behind his back, and into the open doorway. "Because, he lost a lot of blood, and seemed weak."

Todd looks behind him, "He'll be okay." He digs into his pocket and hands me a list. "I need these things to keep him stable though. Most of it's just alcohol, and antibiotics."

I take the list out of his hands. "I'll make sure we get what you need."

"Good," he says. "Once I get the medicine in him, I'm thinking that we'll need to keep him here for three days. I don't know where you all want to take him, but he won't be stable enough to be transported before that timeframe. Okay?"

"I'll let them know."

He places a hand on my shoulder and I jump back. "But, how are you, Porsche? And, what happened to your face? What happened to the other girls' faces too? It looks like you all have been in a big fight." *We did.* I think to myself. *We fought ourselves.* "The only one without scars seems to be...C-Crystal."

He stumbles when he says her name and I wonder why.

"I'm fine," I say in a low voice. "And, with the stitches you got going across your forehead, you need to worry about yourself."

He rubs the stitches in his face that he got from showing some girl his dick. "I earned these."

"I'm worried about Brillo," I say trying to change the topic. "Is he really okay?"

"Look, Porsche, I'm sorry for what I did the last time I saw you," he says looking into my eyes. I look away. "I was high, and tripping hard. I didn't know what I was doing, and it was wrong. But, I'm getting help now."

"Todd, I don't care," I lie. "The only thing we share is blood now."

He lowers his head, and throws the bloody towel over his shoulder. "So I'm Todd now?" He says to me folding his arms over his chest. "I'm not even Uncle Todd anymore?"

"You're still my uncle, I'm just...I'm just hurt," I say turning around and sitting on the sofa. "I don't understand why you would look at me like that."

He closes the bedroom door, and walks over toward me to take a seat. "Baby girl, I hope you don't blame yourself for my actions. That was all on me, not you. Like I said I need help."

"I don't blame myself," I tell him seriously. "I just don't understand how you could see me like that. Mama said you use to change my diapers."

He throws the bloody towel on the table. "How did you get caught up with these girls?" He asks me changing the subject. I'm grateful. "These type of girls aren't you."

"How would you know?" I ask rolling my eyes. I hate that he's trying to act like we're so close. He proved to me a while back, at the store, that he doesn't care about me.

"I know you, Porsche," he says rolling the sleeves up on his white shirt. "These girls are full speed ahead. You need to stay away from them. I been in these streets longer than I care to admit, and I know danger when I see it."

I see track marks all over his arms, from the needles he pushes into his veins. He's addicted to heroin, but I always thought he was on crack.

"I'll be good," I tell him standing up. "I'm going to check on Brillo."

"Before you go, Marcy said she was going to pay me," he rubs his arms. "You know where it is?"

I walk over to the microwave, and grab the baggie on top of it. I pick it up and step up to him. I wonder if this dope is safe, or if it will have the same effect that it had on Dragon. I don't trust Marcy. I don't trust Crystal. But, I know no matter what I say, he will still want it anyway.

I stretch my hand out and say, "It's right here."

He stands up from the couch, takes it out of my hand, and says, "Thank you."

I don't want to see him use it, so I walk toward Brillo's door, open it up, and walk inside. Brillo is looking at *Martin* on TV when I walk inside. It's the episode when Martin is boxing Tommy 'The Hitman' Hearns. Brillo's laughing softly when Martin walks out of his bedroom with a beaten up head.

I love Brillo's laugh. It's so cute. So sweet.

"How are you feeling?" I ask sitting on the bed across from him. "In much pain now?"

He turns around, and looks at me. My heart is beating fast. But, not because I'm scared, or worried or anything like that. But, because I care about him, and for some reason, I like him too.

"I'm feeling better," he says grinning at me.

Why do I feel warm inside?

"Thank you for everything you've done for me," he says in a low voice. "Before, you came to the motel that day, I knew I was going to die. I don't pray to God a lot, but I prayed for help before I saw your face. Thirty minutes later, I saw you."

"Don't lie to me," I say under my breath.

"I'm serious," Brillo says turning the TV sound off with the remote control, using the only hand he has left...his right. "Before you, I was saying my goodbyes to my family, even though I knew they couldn't hear me."

"You want me to let you use a phone?" I ask. "To call for help?"

Where did that come from? I'm risking everything by letting him call home. I've seen first hand the kind of person Marcy is. She won't waste anytime pushing her gun to my temple, and pulling the trigger. So it's dumb for me to ask him such a thing, but its too late. I already put myself out there.

"I'm not going to ask you to do that," Brillo says. "I know they are going to take me back to my family. But, who I'm worried about is you."

"Me," I say pointing to myself.

"Yes you," he tells me. "You don't need to be around them, Porsche."

I love the way he says my name. It sounds like he's singing Porsche, even though he's not.

"Why you worried about me?" I ask him kicking my feet out. "I'm not the one in pain."

"Porsche, you need to get away from them," he tells me. "They are good at what they do. They are ultimate manipulators, and will have you thinking shit is sweet when it isn't. But, the moment you let your guard down, they will cut you. Where it hurts. Get away from them, and do it while you still can. I'll be okay, what I want you to do is go now."

"I can handle myself," I say although I don't believe my own lies.

"Get away from them," he repeats. "Please."

"Why do you care about me so much?" I ask. "You don't even know me."

"Because, you care about me," he says. "I can tell in the way you look at me." He shakes his head. "What's funny is, you look so much like her, yet ya'll couldn't be more different."

"I care about all people," I say.

Why would I say that dumb shit? I'm trying to be cool at the wrong time. I guess that's why I don't have a boyfriend now.

"You can say whatever you want," he continues, but I know you care about me. What I don't know is why?"

I shrug. "I guess its because you lying up here all fucked up and shit," I tell him focusing on the mute TV. "I don't like to see people in pain like you. Plus, you seem like you nice."

"I am nice," he winks at me. "But, I'm also wise, and I want you to listen to me."

"I am listening to you," I say. I love that he's so bossy.

"Listen and hear me good," he says looking into my eyes. "I need you to get out of here. And, I need you to do it as soon as possible."

"I can't do that," I tell him.

"Why not?"

"Because, you're still here. And, I'll worry about you."

I know my answer is dumb, but it's the truth. Even if I were to leave, I would always wonder how he is, and if he made it out okay. I can't go unless I know he's gone too. Even, if it means my life.

"You're serious aren't you?" Brillo asks me.

"Very."

"Well let's do this," he says. "You look out for me, and I'll look out for you."

"Now how are you going to do that?" I say looking at his bloody stump, which is covered with gauze.

"I got an idea, but when the time comes for me to tell you, I need for you to trust me, okay?"

"Okay," I smile.

# SULTRY SUNDAY
# DAY TWELVE
# Chapter Thirty-One

I'm feeding Brillo chicken broth. Once again Marcy, Champagne and Crystal are gone, which means we're all alone. I like it like this. My uncle Todd is in the living room part of the hotel, but he doesn't bother us. Besides, the only thing he cares about is heroin, and I'm glad he has dope as his company.

"Where you live at?" Brillo asks me after I give him a spoonful of broth.

"Lavender Projects," I say in a low voice. "And, before you go there I already know it's a mess. I hate living around there."

"You know the projects don't make you," he says. "You make the projects. If anything you should use the bad experiences you had there as an opportunity to get out, and do something with your life."

"You sound like my mother," I tell him dipping the plastic spoon into the white Styrofoam cup. "But, what you telling me to do is easier said than done."

"So you let what goes on in the projects control your life?" He asks me.

I try to give him another spoonful of broth, but he shakes his head.

"I'm good," he tells me. "My appetite is spoiled."

I sit the cup down on the table, and sit back on the bed across from him. I hate talking about life. Mainly, because I don't have a plan. I don't know what I want to do in life, or who I plan to be.

"I don't let the projects control my life, but all I see everyday is violence and drama," I tell him lying on the bed on my side, so that I'm faced his direction. "My mother tells me all the time that I should lead my own life, but I don't know what life I want to lead."

"What do you like to do?" He asks me.

I think about the past eleven days I've spent with the Drunk and Hot girls. I drink everyday, which I love. I've had sex with multiple men, which I can do without. And, I live day by day. None of the things I've experienced can be profitable in the long run, but it's the most fun I've ever had in my life. Plus I'm looking into the eyes of a man I believe is for me.

"Nothing," I shrug my shoulders. "I don't like to do nothing I guess."

I'm so dumb and whack. Why would anybody want to fuck with me? I don't got no life. I don't got no brain.

"Come on," he says weakly, still with that cute smile on his face. "Think…there has to be something that you enjoy doing."

"I like helping people," I say truthfully. "I like adventure."

His eyes widen. "Then you can be a travel advisor," Brillo says excitedly. "Or, a travel consultant. Maybe you can travel around the world. People who don't mind traveling have a lot of options. Maybe, you could learn another language. You see what I'm saying?" He says. "You can do anything you want. You just gotta choose."

I smile.

"Hey, what was your plan for your life?" I ask him. "Before, you got like this."

He's frowning now. Well, not really frowning...he looks sadder than anything.

"I was saving my money," he says looking out of the window. "I wanted to open a gym. I loved to lift weights and stuff like that. I didn't want to get extra bulky, or nothing. I wanted to work with overweight people who struggled to get their lives back on track. I wanted to be a motivational trainer." He raises his left stump. "I guess I can't do that now right?"

"You can do anything you want," I say getting up and approaching his bed. I sit on the edge, and place my hand on his arm. "Plus you can get a prosthetic now, and everything. You'll be fine."

"How the fuck would you know?" Crystal asks walking into the room. "You don't know shit about my man."

I jump up. I'm staring into my face. Except it's not my face...it's the bitch who's man I'm trying to steal.

"I didn't say I knew him –"

"Crystal, ease up," Brillo says to her. "We were just talking about something that you came in on the tail end of."

"Is that right?" Crystal asks sitting on his bed.

When I look at Brillo's face I notice he seems uneasy, with her so close to him. Like he has an attitude or something.

"How about you share with me what you both were talking about," Crystal says looking into my eyes. "Go ahead," she continues. "I'm listening. How do you know he will be fine, Porsche?"

I clench my fists. "It was nothing," I tell her sternly. "Just drop it already."

"I'm glad it was nothing, but let me make something clear," she places her hand on his stomach. "Whether he's broken or not, this nigga belongs to me. You understand what I mean? He is mine."

"I don't belong to nobody," Brillo tells her right away.

She turns around and looks down at him. "Is that right?" She crosses her leg, and shakes her right foot rapidly. "Because, if you don't belong to me, I don't have no reason to keep you around right? And, if I don't have no reason to keep you around, I can dispose of you as I see fit. So you want to tell me again that you don't belong to me?"

When I hear she's going to dispose of him I get faint. "Crystal, He didn't mean it like that—"

She puts her hand up to silence me.

"Brillo, are you my man or not?" She asks him.

He doesn't respond. And, I feel bad that I put him in this situation, by being in here. I don't know why I can't stay out of his room. Marcy, Champagne and Crystal are always gone, and it leaves us with time alone. I enjoy talking to him, and he enjoys talking to me. But, if I'm going to put his life in danger, I won't come in here anymore.

"Hear me good," Crystal says looking at me. "Your name is Porsche." She points at me. "My name is Crystal." She points at herself. "Now you played my stunt double for a long time, but the real bitch has now returned. And, I don't want you sniffing around what belongs to me, and that includes my man, his dick, and my friends. Understand?"

"I understand."

I turn around and walk out of the door. My heart aches. I want her dead. When I close the door I'm standing in front of Champagne."

"How you doing?" She asks handing me a drink.

"Fine I guess," I say taking a sip, and sitting on the sofa. "Were you able to get the things on the list that my uncle Todd needs? I gave the list to Marcy yesterday, but earlier when my uncle was here he said he still didn't have the things from the pharmacy."

"I'm sure she's going to handle it," Champagne says standing in front of me. "You care about him don't you?" She nods at the bedroom door. "Brillo."

I frown. "I don't want Brillo hurt if that's what you mean." I look away from her, so that she can't see the lies in my eyes. "I don't think your friend likes me though. She told me to stay away from Brillo, and her friends just now."

"I don't give a fuck who she likes, or what she thinks," Champagne says sitting next to me. "Because, of her I don't have a family."

I've been so caught up with Brillo, that I forgot she suffered several losses.

"How are you doing?" I ask sincerely.

"I'm holding up, but I don't know how much longer I can do it," she leans back into the sofa, and stares up at the ceiling. "I just want all of this to be over, so I can start my own life."

I think about the conversation I had with Crystal, outside of the mall. Right after I slashed her tires. Crystal told me about the conversation that she had with them about my business. I remember my feelings being hurt, because they were talking behind my back.

"Why did you tell Crystal about what White Daddy did to me?" I sit the cup down on the table. "I know it's petty, but it hurt my feelings that little time you spoke to her, was spent on me."

Champagne looks sorry. "I told you already, I didn't tell her anything about you. It was Marcy. And, I know it was wrong, but that's what my friends are about. I told you that. It's all about themselves. Now I don't fight with Crystal, because I want her to think shit is cool, until we get our money for handing in Brillo. But, you gotta know I care about you. That's why they mad at me now."

I remember what Brillo said about me not trusting them. If Champagne is lying she's pretty damn good at it. "How do I know I can trust you?"

"Because, I let you go," she says to me. "Remember? I told you, that you could go home. It was Marcy who went to your house, and pulled you back into this shit."

"But, what about what Marcy said? That day when we were all fighting?" I pause. "She said you are going to pawn me off as Crystal, and save your friends."

"That won't be happening," Champagne says with an evil look on her face. "Nobody is using you as a pawn for shit. Crystal has to finally answer for her own drama, and what she did to Brillo."

"Why you say that?" I ask.

"Because, we need Crystal to meet with Axe. He wants her badly for Brillo going missing for so long. Crystal don't know the plans he has for her. She thinks Axe won't hurt her, because she's Brillo's girlfriend. Marcy and I are going to meet with Axe to hand Crystal over," Champagne continues. "But, if for some reason Axe doesn't kill her, you and I will kill her ourselves."

# Chapter Thirty-Two

I'm frozen, and can't move my legs. I'm watching my uncle Todd carry Brillo's naked limp body in his arms.

"Porsche, wake up," Todd yells at me. "Open the bathroom door. You can't keep standing over there looking crazy. I need your help."

I snap out of it, and rush to the bathroom. I open the door, and watch Todd put him into the tub of water, which is filled with ice cubes.

Brillo's eyes aren't opening. And, he doesn't seem responsive. I feel all-alone. I feel helpless. What can I do now?

"Porsche, his fever is through the roof right now," Todd says to me while I stand in the middle of the bathroom floor, and observe Brillo's weak face. "Did you get the things I needed on the list?"

"What list?" I say.

I don't know what's going on.

"The list, Porsche," he repeats. "The list I told you I needed to keep his infections under control. Where are the things?"

My mind is racing, and I try to slow it down. I go back to the day he handed me the list. It was Saturday. Now it's Sunday, and Brillo is sick, and we still don't have what we need to save his life. They are so trifling.

"I gave the list to Marcy," I tell him. "She told me she would get the things. She probably didn't get them."

"Fuck," Todd yells. "Go into the room and get me a sheet of paper and a pen."

I look at Brillo. My feet are glued to the floor. I can't move.

"Porsche, wake the fuck up," Todd screams at me. "Now go into the room, and bring me a pen and a pad. It's on the dresser."

I run to the room. I look at the bed sheets on the floor that were once on Brillo's bed. I'm scared for Brillo. I'm scared for us. It's not only because I love Brillo. But, because if Brillo dies today all of our lives are in danger. And, now since my uncle Todd is involved, that means his life too.

"Porsche, bring me the pen and the paper," my uncle yells at me from the bathroom. "Hurry the fuck up!"

I snap out of it, and grab what he needs. I move toward the bathroom again. I can hear the water sloshing back and forth in the tub.

When I make it to the bathroom, I give him the sheet of paper. He dries his hands off, and writes down a bunch of things.

I try not to look at Brillo's dick, because I know he's in a terrible position, but I do anyway. He's big, even though he's soft, and I understand why Crystal is tripping so hard.

"Here," my uncle says breaking my lustful stare. "I need you to get everything on this list. Now some of the things you have to buy you'll need a prescription for. If you go to the pharmacy in Lavender Projects, and ask for George. He'll give you what you need if you tell him it's for me. He used to work at the pharmacy when I ran my practice. But, you gonna have to pay him a lot."

My eyes widen. "I don't have no money. You got any on you?"

"Honey, I'm broke," he says. "I don't get my check until next week some time."

"But, what if I can't get this?"

My uncle looks back at Brillo's limp body. "Then your friend will die today."

"But, he can't die," I cry.

"I'm sorry, honey. I truly am. But, there is nothing else I can do. I need the things on that list."

My heart beats fast. I'm not losing Brillo tonight, and I don't care what I have to do. It's kind of messed up that Marcy, Champagne and Crystal knew I don't have no money, and didn't leave me with none. The only thing they kept talking about was how I shook my ass at the bar for 15 bucks, and lost $1,000. Get over it already.

My uncle turns around, drops to his knees, and works on Brillo. I take a look at the list he gave me. It has stuff like Penicillin and Tylenol on it. But, when I see he also added a $50.00 bag of dope, I get mad.

Frowning I say, "What's this?"

He stands up, and looks at where my finger is pointing. "That's my fee," he says getting back on his knees to wipe Brillo's body with the cold water. "I might not be in practice anymore, but I damn sure don't work for free. Get me everything on that list, and that includes my dope. I love you, baby girl, but I don't play when it comes to my habit. You need to know that."

# Chapter Thirty-Three

Before I left the hotel I called George at the Pharmacy in Lavender Projects. He told me that for everything on the list I would need $500. I don't have a dime. So, I am standing in front of the pharmacy, trying to do anything I can to get the money, and that includes fucking. But, nobody bites. Maybe the wild look in my eyes when I ask if anybody wants to fuck is turning folks off.

When I see an older white man walk into the pharmacy with a younger black girl, I get an idea. If it works I'll save Brillo's life. If it doesn't I will have made a big mistake.

I'm sitting in White Daddy's Rav 4, a few blocks from the pharmacy. I guess he didn't want to drive one of his nicer cars from Philadelphia to Maryland. I don't blame him.

"I'm glad you called me," White Daddy says rubbing the back of my head. "I miss that pretty face of yours."

"I miss your face too," I lie. "But, I need to tell you something first," I say. "My name is Porsche, not Crystal."

"I know," he says. "I knew the first moment I saw you, but I decided to play your game. I was going to let you carry the charade on for as long as you wanted to."

I smile.

"I feel dumb," I admit.

"Don't," he says rubbing my chin with the back of his hand. "Anyway, I have been thinking about you ever since you left my house. How have you been?"

"Not too good," I say trying to find a good way to beg for money. "How have you been?"

"Busy I guess," he says rubbing my meaty thigh. "With all of the apartment buildings I own on the east coast, my life can be hectic." He looks out in front of him. "I need an escape every chance I get." He sighs. "Who do you live with?"

"My mother," I say hating to talk about her. "We live in the projects."

"What a shame," he says in a low voice. "A pretty thing like you should have a prettier place to rest your head. I can do that for you, if you let me."

I don't want him doing anything else for me, but giving me some money. I need to get Brillo's medicine. But, I can't just come out and say it. If I do he might catch on to the real reason I wanted him here, and cut me off. I still remember how he acted with Marcy when she asked for her money.

"I'm use to staying with my mother now," I tell him. "In the projects so, it's not that bad. Plus I got plans and goals when it's finally time for me to leave."

His eyebrows rise. "You do?" He sits back in the driver's seat and crosses his arms over his chest. "Tell me about them."

Aw shit. I done ran game, and now he's calling me on it.

"I want to travel," I say remembering what me, and Brillo talked about. "I want to be a consultant for people who travel abroad, but might need help."

He laughs. "Sweetheart, what do you know about traveling? You probably haven't been out of the country."

He sounds like he's talking down to me, and it makes me angry. I don't know which fork to use when I eat at a fine restaurant. I don't know nothing about how to run a business. But, I have seen some parts of the world thanks to my mother. And, I'm not just talking about the east coast that Marcy and Champagne so graciously showed me lately.

"For awhile, I lived in Paris," I say scratching my scalp. I feel like a monkey so I put my hands in my lap.

"You lived in Paris?" His laugh is so heavy, the inside of my ears itch. "You are a very sweet girl, but whatever you do, please don't become a liar like that Marcy or Champagne. That's one of the things I hate about them. They aren't honest. You have not lived in Paris, young lady."

"Je ne suis pas un menteur," I say to him in French. In English it means, 'I am not a liar'.

His eyes widen, and his jaw drops. I knew I was going to rock him, but I didn't expect his response to be so dramatic.

"Parlez-vous francais?" He responds. He's asking me do I speak French.

"Oui," I say. Which means '*Yes*' in French. "Je parle francais couramment. J'yi ai vecu pendant une grande partie de ma vie." In English I said, 'I speak French fluently. I lived there for a large part of my life.'

"I think I fell in love with you harder," he says looking at me as if I'm another woman. "I apologize for assuming you were lying."

"It's okay," I say. "But, I need your help."

"Anything," he tells me.

His entire mood has changed. I guess in his eyes there's nothing sexier than a black girl who speaks French.

"I need $500," I tell him. "Right away."

Instead of beating around the bush I decide to come out with it. Besides, I can tell he feels bad for assuming that just because I'm Porsche from up the block, that I'm not worldly. I'm going to be honest about something else too. Before, this moment it never occurred to me that I'm not as non-essential as I believed all my life.

Going to Paris when most of the people in my town haven't been out of the city, means that I have seen the world. And, knowing another language makes me more valuable than I realize. Maybe, Brillo is right. He has me wanting to be a better person already. And, I have to save his life.

"Why you want the money?" White Daddy asks me.

"Because, I asked you for it," I respond. "Are you gonna give it to me or not?"

At this point I have nothing to lose. He'll either give me the money, and I'll go save Brillo's life, or he won't and I'll find another way to make the paper. Whatever he decides, I don't have the time to be sitting in the passenger seat of his Rav 4, wondering what the verdict will be.

"I'll do it," he says pulling his wallet out of his pocket. "But, I want to spend some more time with you too." He separates five crisp one hundred dollar bills from the stack, and hand them to me.

"Not a problem," I reply taking the money. "After I make a stop, I'll come meet you." I raise my butt off of the seat, and stuff the money in my back jean pocket. "Where are you going to be later on?"

"I'm not playing that game," he says shaking his head from left to right.

"What do you mean?" I ask him.

"Marcy and you girls love playing with me and taking my money," he responds. He's on that bullshit again, with lumping me with Marcy and them. "So either you take me with you, or give me my money back."

For him to be so professional, and make so much money, he sure is acting very weak. He acts like he's trying to fall in love with me, instead of just getting some pussy. Maybe I went too far by speaking to him in French.

"I'm gonna be honest with you," I say positioning myself so that I can look directly into his eyes. "I am staying in a hotel, and it's overcrowded. A friend of mine is in a tub suffering from a bad fever, and he needs my help. So, you can't go with me. And, I don't have anywhere to take you. So, I was kind of hoping that you would get us a room, and we could play together later."

"I got a better idea," he pulls down the zipper on his jeans. "How about you earn that money in your pocket right now." He releases his big pink penis. "And, take me with you later. After we help your friend, I'll get a room, and we can have a little more fun together."

At first I frown at his dick, until I see the irritation on his face.

"Are you going to take care of me or what?"

I frown again, but lower my head like a crane. Before, I know it his entire penis is in my mouth. For some reason I think about Brillo. I wonder would he do the same thing for me, if he were in my situation. When I remember that White Daddy is a man, and so is Brillo, I realize I don't want him to return the favor. Besides, Brillo doesn't know how I feel about him. He doesn't know about all of the crazy things, I think about him in my mind.

I bend down and suck him into my throat. When I feel myself gagging, I cough hard, and lower my neck again. He pushes down on my head with his palm. I find it hard to breathe now. And just when I think he's taking most of my breath, he takes the rest of my air, when he pushes his dick deeper into my throat. I cough harder, grab some air, and go back in.

"That's good, Crystal," he tells me. "You being a good little girl right now."

Since he knows my name, I wonder why he calls me by hers? I don't say anything to him though. I just handle my business. I suck him into my throat, jerk his dick, and spit on it repeatedly, just the way I saw Marcy do him at his house. The difference is, it takes him no time to cum with me. Before he spits his cream on my tongue, I lift my head, so it won't go into my mouth. I do it just before he squirts into my hand. His cum rolls over my finger like hot lava coming out of a volcano.

"Damn," he says looking at me. "I like you."

I smile. "Can you take me to the pharmacy?" I say. I don't feel like much of the games anymore. "I really got to get back to the hotel."

We make it back to the hotel just in time to help Brillo. I'm not surprised that Marcy, Champagne and Crystal are not back though. White Daddy sits in the living room, and I go to Brillo's room to check on him. I'm secretly hoping that White Daddy will leave. I don't want Brillo to know he's here, or that I just sucked his dick for some medicine.

After some time, my uncle Todd brings Brillo's fever under control.

"You did good," Todd tells me removing a thermometer from Brillo's mouth. He looks at it. "His fever is going down." He sits the thermometer down on the table.

I look at Brillo. He opens his eyes and he smiles at me.

"What you looking at me like that for, girl?" he says. "You like something you see over here?"

My heart rattles. The way he called me girl sounds so cool.

"I'm looking at you, because these are my eyes," I say sitting on the edge of his bed. "And, I use them. How do you feel?

"Better," he responds. "And, your uncle told me it was because of you. I appreciate everything, Porsche."

"It's no problem," I say. "I'll do it again if I have too."

"You got anything for me," Todd says looking down at us.

I give him $50, since I didn't feel like copping no heroin. "Since he's good, I'm going to hit these streets now," Todd says to me. "Thank you for the money."

He stuffs the money into his pocket, and walks out of the room. I'm glad he closes the door, because White Daddy is sitting in there, and I want some more alone time with Brillo.

When my uncle is gone I say, "Don't do that to me anymore, Brillo. I was worried sick about you."

Brillo closes his eyes, and shakes his head. "I'm surprised I'm even still alive," he sighs. "You got to remember, I don't have one of my hands, Porsche. My body isn't operating to its fullest potential. That's why I know this bitch is certified. She don't think about shit like that."

"I know," I say rubbing my temples. "Sometimes I forget because you seem so strong."

"I am strong, mama," he winks. "But, even the strongest man gets weak sometimes." He looks into my eyes. "Thank you so much for being here for me. I mean it."

Before I can reply I hear the front door close real hard. "Give me a second, Brillo," I say to him standing up. "I have to see what's going on out there."

When I open the door, and walk into the living room, I see Marcy standing behind White Daddy's head. She's holding a gun out of his view. Champagne and Crystal stand on her side. Although, Crystal is smiling, Champagne seems to be angry with her.

"I'm glad you called White Daddy, Porsche," Marcy tells me. "I was running out of money. And, this is just the hit that we needed."

I know right away what that means. He's about to die.

Poor White Daddy.

# MEANINGFUL MONDAY
# DAY THIRTEEN
# Chapter Thirty-Four

When I got up this morning, there was no Marcy, Champagne or Crystal in the hotel. And, there was blood on the spot where White Daddy was sitting on the sofa. I know they did something with his body. They kill people like it's nothing.

My head is ringing this morning, probably because I popped one of Marcy's sleeping pills to catch a good night's sleep. Marcy takes the pills most nights, but I only take them when my mind won't allow me to get some rest.

My uncle is not here, and I'm sitting in the living room portion of the suite. I keep looking at the closed door where Brillo is resting. I'm trying to give him some time to sleep, before I bother him. But, after fifteen minutes I realize I can't take it anymore. I have to see his face.

I walk to the door, and knock lightly.

"Come in," Brillo says to me.

I walk in, and close the door behind me. "How do you feel?" I ask looking at his body. He's wrapped up in a white sheet, but thankfully he looks much better than yesterday. He's the color of honey, and so cute.

"I'm better," he smiles. "No matter what I do, I feel like I can never thank you enough."

I walk over to his bed, and place my hand on his wet clammy forehead. He feels a little warm, so I go to the bathroom, and fill the ice bucket with cool water from the sink. I grab a rag, walk back into the room, and close the door behind me.

"You can't die on me," I say to him, sitting on the edge of his bed. "After, everything I had to do to save your life, if you die, it would be for nothing." I dip the rag into the cool water, and rub it softly on his forehead.

"What you have to do?" He asks me. He looks concerned. "I hope you didn't compromise yourself. I don't want that life for you. I care about you too much."

I think about how White Daddy's dick rested on my tonsils yesterday. And, I think about how his cum spilled over my fingers, after he reached an orgasm.

"I didn't compromise myself," I smile. "My dignity is still in tact."

"I doubt that," he laughs. He looks into my eyes. "I'm going to tell my brother about you."

My eyes widen, and the rag drops out of my hand, and falls on the pillow next to his head. I thought he liked me. So why is he going to tell his brother on me. "What did I do?" I'm shivering again.

"It's not like that," he says to me. His voice is heavy with concern. "I'm going to tell Axe how you looked out for me. I'm going to tell him that when shit got rough, you wouldn't let me die."

I'm smiling now.

"Can you do something for me though?" He asks me seriously.

I nod my head up and down quickly, and my teeth rattle. "Anything." I don't tell him, but *anything* in my book includes sucking his dick.

"Can you get that cold rag off of my ear you just dropped?"

I laugh hard, and grip my stomach. It's the first good laugh I had in a long time. He makes me smile. *Oh God, I want him so badly.*

I take the rag off of his pillow, remove the wet pillow from under his head, and replace it with a dry pillow from the other bed. Then I dip the rag back into the cool water, and rub his head again.

"Thank you for being nice to me," I say looking into his eyes. "People aren't usually nice to me."

"Then that's their problem," he says to me. "Don't make it yours."

"I'm getting better with that," I say rubbing his head with the wet rag again.

He reaches over and touches my hand with his right hand. Chills run through my body. "Porsche, Axe is not going to like what's gone on here," he looks at his left arm, where his hand use to be. "So, you have to stay away from them. They are good with making you think you are in their circle, but the only people they care about is each other. Marcy, Champagne and Crystal are some sort of cult, and you shouldn't believe anything them bitches say to you."

"I don't have any intentions on being around them after they take you home tomorrow," I say. "I was thinking about going home later tonight, and everything."

"No," he says. "I want you to meet my brother. I want to clear up your name. And, I want him to know that you alone got me through this shit. If I don't tell him the truth, they will lie on you, trust me. I know them. Please don't trust them bitches," he says seriously. "I mean it, Porsche. Do you promise me?"

"I promise. I won't trust them."

He smiles. "Good, and Axe is gonna take care of you and your uncle financially for everything you did for me."

"I don't want your money," I frown. "I just want you out of here, and well."

"I know," he winks. "That's why I like you, and am going to hook you up anyway." His voice grows serious again. "Porsche, how old are you?"

"Eighteen," I lie.

"No you not," he smiles. "What are you, about sixteen or something?"

Since he was pushing my age too far back I decide to be honest. "I'm seventeen, but I'll be eighteen next month."

"Then I'll wait for you," he says in a voice that makes me tingle in my gooey place.

"You'll wait for her where?" Crystal says coming into the room. Her face is painted up, which means she and the other two must've been out selling pussy somewhere. "Enlighten me on what you are going to wait for her to do."

"I didn't say I'll wait for her," he responds. "I said I need a break."

The way Crystal's forehead wrinkles lets me know that she doesn't believe him. She walks toward me, and I stand up, and place the wet bucket and rag on the dresser.

"I'll leave you two alone," I say walking around her.

Before I reach the door she says, "I won't let you have him."

I turn around and look into her eyes. "I don't know what you're talking about," I respond.

"Yes you do, Porsche," she says approaching me. "I won't let you have him. He belongs to me. I worked too hard to keep him." She starts laughing. "I mean think about it for a second. Look at all of the trouble I've gone through." Crystal looks back at Brillo. "I fucking cut his hand off. Do you actually think that I will allow you to keep him? After everything that I did?"

"I think you got the wrong impression about me and Brillo's friendship," I start. "Brillo is sick, and since you and your friends don't seem interested in making sure he gets better, I got to do it alone."

"You don't got to do shit," she says walking so close to me that our breasts bump.

"I do," I say trying not to show my fright. "If I didn't he could've died."

If I thought she would fight me straight up, I might not be so scared. But, I've been around them long enough to know that they are killers.

"If he gonna die, then let him," she says. "But, I don't want you around him, even if it means seeing him at his grave."

I look at Brillo. He seems to be calm, but I know that his feelings are hurt.

"I'm gone," I say walking out the door. I close it behind me.

"Just remember what I said," Crystal says to my back.

When I'm out the door, I see my uncle. He looks high. He's on the sofa, watching the TV, which is turned off. I can see the empty syringe on the brown table. A drop of blood dangles from the tip of the needle, and threatens to fall on the table.

"You had an aunt," Todd says to me. "She was your mother's twin sister. She was also my sister."

My jaw drops, and I take a seat next to him. I'm waiting for his next sentence, but he doesn't say anything. He nods off. So, I place my hand on his dirty blue jeans. "Uncle Todd, what are you talking about?"

"Your mother had a twin," he says waking up. "She was identical to your mother." He smiles at the TV, and a long drool of spit oozes down the left side of his mouth. It stretches, and dangles until it drops onto his dirty white t-shirt. "They were so close, and where you saw one, you saw the other."

He's quiet again, and I slap him so hard on his cheek that his eyes pop open. "Finish telling me," I yell at him.

"One day your mother, and your father got into a fight," he continues. "It was a bad fight." His head dips back, and I hope he doesn't nod off again. "David hit her in the eye, and almost destroyed her eye socket. You were about three years old when it happened."

I remember that day. It was the last day I saw my father's white face. My mother, and father were fighting, and she was holding her eye with one hand, and the door with the other. She made him leave. My daddy kissed me on the face, and I remember him smelling like alcohol. I didn't want him to go.

"Your aunt Felicia went over to David's house to confront him about what he did to her twin sister," he continues. "To my sister." His head drops. "Your mother asked me to go stop her, but I didn't want to." In a lower voice he says, "I was scared. I knew the killer David was. He was born that way. Some people are born killers."

He stops talking again, and I stand up and look down at him. He's a mess. His clothes are dingy, and his arms have track marks running up and down them. I hate him so much right now.

"Finish," I say in a serious tone.

"When Felicia went to approach David, he beat her to death, with his bare hands," Todd is crying now. "And he dumped her body in a trash dump, in his apartment building. He was arrested after awhile, and is still doing time in federal prison."

I can't believe all of this. My body is so stiff I can't move.

"Felicia had a daughter, about two years older than you," he continues. "The streets said David's mother took her, and it may be true. But whenever we went to the cops, and asked about the baby, they investigated his family. The baby was never there. I never knew what happened to my niece, until you called me to this hotel, to help your friend, and I saw Crystal."

My jaw drops. "So, Crystal is my cousin?" My bottom lip hangs lower. "But, how can you be sure?"

"I know my niece when I see her," he responds. "Plus she looks just like you. Her name is different, but that's her. The funny thing is, she has no idea who you are. I'm sure of it." He stands up, and walks to the front door. "Had I defended your mother, both of them would be alive today. And, Crystal wouldn't be the kind of person she is." He walks out of the room, leaving me stunned.

I don't have a chance to regroup because Marcy and Champagne reenter the room the moment he leaves.

"What's wrong with you?" Marcy asks me, holding a paper bag in her arms. "You look like you seen a ghost." She sits the bag on the table.

I don't respond.

"Yeah, Porsche," Champagne says sitting her red Gucci on the table, next to my uncle's bloody syringe. "Why you standing in the middle of the floor looking crazy?"

I can't open my mouth.

"I'm going in there to check on Brillo," Marcy says laughing at me. "I'll leave you both to it."

Champagne and I are alone now. Champagne places a hand on my shoulder. "Are you fine?"

"Yes," I say nodding my head up and down.

"You know we take Brillo to Axe tomorrow right?" She asks me. I can smell the liquor on her breath. "You still with the plan?"

"What plan?" I ask. The only thing on my mind right now is Crystal and our relation to each other.

"We are going to kill Crystal tomorrow," Champagne says. "I know you think everything is cool with us, because I been hanging out with them lately, but I had to front. Brillo is giving us $40,000 tomorrow. Me and Marcy are gonna give you $10,000, and split the rest." She grips both of my arms and pulls me toward her. "This is almost over. After, Crystal faces Axe for what she did to Brillo; we will be able to get back to our own lives. And, if Axe doesn't kill Crystal, me and you will do it ourselves."

Now that I know Crystal is related to me, I guess I should be against the murder. But, I'm not, because I don't like what she represents, just like I don't like my uncle Todd, and what he stands for.

I look into Champagnes eyes. "I'm with whatever you got planned," I tell her. "I just want this shit over, and for that bitch to get everything she deserves."

# TERRIBLE TUESDAY
# DAY FOURTEEN
# Chapter Thirty-Five

Somebody is fighting in my dreams. When I open my eyes and turn over on the sofa I sleep on in the hotel, I realize its Champagne and Marcy. They are in the middle of the living room floor pushing each other and arguing back and forth.

"Why the fuck would you let her leave?" Champagne says to Marcy shoving her toward the TV. "We came this far for nothing."

Marcy rams Champagne, and she falls into my lap. For a moment, I loose breath.

"Bitch, don't try to put this shit on me," Marcy yells pointing at Champagne. "How the fuck did I know she would leave in the middle of the night?"

"Well if you stop popping those sleeping pills like mints you would've heard her creep out the door," Champagne says to her standing up.

I can breathe better now.

"Where the fuck was you at last night?" Marcy responds placing both hands on her hips. "Had you not been with that nigga who kicks your ass every other month, you would've been here to stop her."

"I wasn't with Desmond," Champagne says walking away. "I don't know what you're talking about."

"Sure you do, bitch," Marcy says walking up behind her. "If you wasn't with Desmond last night, then that means I never bust my gun."

Well we all know that ain't true, so Champagne must be lying.

When Todd comes out of the door holding Brillo's limp body in his arms I jump up. "Open the door," he tells Champagne who rushes and opens it.

"I got it." Champagne holds the door open. "The car is out front, Todd. You can put him in the backseat. We coming down in a minute to take him to Axe."

"What is wrong with Brillo?" I ask trying to follow my uncle out of the room.

Champagne stops my movements with a stiff hand to the middle of my chest. She closes the door and says, "Everything cool. He's sleep."

I'm crying. Tears are filling up in my eyes, and I can't see her face, because she looks blurry. I don't believe her. I don't believe he is alive. "What's wrong with him?" I ask. "Why he dead?"

"Because, he's sleep," Champagne says. "You gotta trust me. What we look like taking him back to his brother dead? Use your head, Porsche. Would we have gone through all of this, just to kill him? It doesn't make logical sense."

Marcy walks over to me and says, "But, there is another problem we have to consider, since Crystal is gone."

"What problem?" I wipe the water off of my face with the back of my hand.

"Since Crystal left, we need you to meet with Axe," Champagne says to me in a soft voice. "Don't worry though, everything will be okay. Trust me."

"Brillo is dead," I say shaking my head. "I'm not meeting Axe with Brillo being dead." I cry again, but just a little harder this time.

"On everything I love, he is sleep," Champagne says. "He's not fucking dead. So, stop saying that shit."

When my uncle comes back into the room without Brillo, I rush toward him. "Uncle Todd, is Brillo dead? Is he okay? He looked dead." My mind is moving a mile a minute, along with my lips.

"Dead?" he frowns. "That boy is in the car sleep." He's laughing. "What made you think something like that?"

"Because, he looked limp when you had him in your arms," I say feeling a little better. After all, why would my uncle lie?

"The boy has been through everything, Porsche," my uncle says to me. "He's just tired, Baby girl. I been up with him all night. Trust me when I say that he's fine. Saving his life proved to me that I still have it."

He places a hand on my shoulder, and I walk back from him. I'm not too comfortable with him laying hands on me quite yet.

Todd says, "I'm sorry for touching you, Porsche." In a softer voice he says, "Don't worry about Brillo. He's a strong young man, and he's alright. I've given him all that I have. You can trust me."

I believe him now.

"Good, since we got that out of the way, come back here later on tonight," Marcy says to my uncle. "I'll give you the money for everything you did for Brillo, plus a little bit more."

I know what she really wants to do to my uncle, and I won't let it happen. I don't like my uncle's freakish ways, but I don't want him dead either.

"That's okay," I say to Marcy. "I'll take care of my uncle out of the money you're going to give me. Uncle Todd, you can just meet me at the house later."

My uncle smiles and shrugs. "As long as I'm getting paid, I could care less who gives me the payout." He walks toward the door. "I'll see you later on," he smiles at me. "I love you." He walks out of the door.

When the three of us are alone Marcy looks at me and says, "You are smart. I guess you been hanging around me too long."

"I can't let you hurt my uncle," I say to her. "He saved Brillo, and deserves to live."

"I'm not going to bother him," Marcy says. "But, I was gonna put something hot in that head. You know I hate witnesses." She's grinning. "As long as you both keep your mouths closed, you're alright in my book." She walks to the door. "Now lets get out of here. It's time to meet Axe, and get this shit over with."

# Chapter Thirty-Six

We are in a small house in Maryland. I know this can't be Axe's main house, because it seems too plain inside. Marcy, Champagne and me are all in the bedroom, looking down at Brillo's sleeping body on a big king size bed. Three doctors are working feverishly on Brillo, and it makes me rest easy.

Brillo is still alive. I am so happy because he's still alive!

Axe turns around and looks at the three of us. He's as scary as I thought he would be. He's over six feet tall, and is as black as an unwashed tire. He must have some kind of Psoriasis, because white particles are all over the collar of his black Polo shirt. And, in his knotty-hair. He's nowhere near as handsome as Brillo, and I wonder how they could be related.

"Thanks for saving his life," Axe says to Marcy and Champagne. "I don't know what I would do without my kid brother. Before my mother died, because her breasts were poisoned, I made a promise to take care of him. I thought I wasn't going to be able to when I heard he was missing, and that would've killed me."

He looks at me like he wants to hurt me.

"Let's go into the living room, to give him some rest," he says.

I look at Brillo, before we leave. I need him to wake up, and tell his brother the truth. He's been sleep for hours now, and I don't know why. When we were at the hotel, he would sleep some, but at some point he would get up, and talk to me. It's like…it's like…it's like he was drugged.

I'm stiff now as I walk into the living room. I know exactly what's going on now. Marcy drugged him, probably with her sleeping pills. She didn't want Brillo telling Axe about me not being the real Crystal.

This entire thing is a set up. Crystal left the hotel on purpose, knowing that I would go in her place. And, they drugged Brillo, knowing that he would tell Axe the truth about me, and they wouldn't get the money. I'm about to die. I'm really about to die.

Axe looks at me and says, "Sit down." He motions to a brown leather recliner across the room.

I take a seat, and place my hands in my lap. He sits on the sofa across from me, and Marcy and Champagne take a seat on his sides.

I look at Champagne again. It's like the veil has been lifted now, and she's showing me who she truly is. Her grin is as conniving as Marcy's. They set me up. Brillo tried to warn me, but now it's too late. This is what it was all about. I'm being sacrificed to save their friend's life. I guess Champagne forgave Crystal for her family being murdered. They are like a cult. They are crazy.

"I didn't do this, Axe," I say as tears roll down my face. "I didn't hurt Brillo."

He laughs and looks to his left at Marcy. "Is your girl serious?"

Marcy sits back into the seat and crosses her legs. She rubs her red manicured nails over the thighs of her black tight jeans. "She is very serious, which is why I don't fuck with her anymore. She's not willing to face the music. Crystal, stop lying to this man. It's too late now."

"Listen to me," I say sitting up in the recliner. "I am not who you think I am. I am not Crystal. You are being played out of your money. Trust me. They are sacrificing me to save their friend, and if you wait on Brillo to wake up he'll tell you everything."

"Is that right?" Axe responds sarcastically. "Well, if you aren't his girlfriend, then who the fuck are you?"

There is a knock at the door, and Axe looks to his right at Champagne. "Go open that for me," he instructs her.

Champagne stands up, and struts toward the front door. Her ass cheeks look like the seats of a seesaw going up and down in her blue jeans.

When the door opens I see Nita, Brillo's sister, and the same girl who pulled a gun on me the first day Champagne scooped me up on the block. My heart is thumping wildly in my chest now.

Champagne sits next to Axe again.

"You came just in time, Nita," Axe says to her as she stands in the middle of the floor, while looking at me. I can smell onions on her skin, like she just had a sub sandwich. "Is this the same chick you saw in the hotel the first day? Is this Crystal?"

Nita looks at me from head to toe. "Yep," Nita nods. Her beefy neck jiggles. "This the bitch right here."

"Well she just told me that she's not the same girl," Axe laughs from the sofa.

"Well this bitch is lying, and trying to play you for a fool," Nita responds. "I might not have known who she was before, but after I saw her that one time in the hotel, I can tell you every mole on her nose now with my eyes closed. This is Crystal," she says pointing at me. "This is Brillo's current girlfriend."

"Why you lying?" Axe says to me. "Why not tell the truth? And, die with some honor?"

"Okay, okay," I say breathing heavily. "I know what this looks like. But, if you wait until Brillo gets up, he will tell you the truth. He'll tell you that I'm not really Crystal. He'll tell you that she was the one who cut his hand off, and that she didn't care whether he lived or died. I'm the one who stayed behind to save his life," I say pointing at my chest. "It was me alone, not them," I point at Champagne and Marcy, "Please believe me."

"I can't take this anymore," Nita says walking toward the kitchen behind me. "I'm about to grab a drink."

Tears are running down my face. But, as usual I know nobody cares.

"Let me ask you something, do you love my brother?" Axe asks me. "I'm going to be honest, your answer doesn't really matter. Your eyes will tell me the truth."

I can't talk. I don't know what to say. Yes I love him, that's why I'm here. That's why I didn't run when I had the chance.

"Answer the question," Champagne says grinning again. "Are you in love with Brillo or not?"

Sweat is rolling out of my hairline, and onto my eyebrows. I wipe it away, but I know they already have seen it. I look at the three of them. Marcy, Champagne and Axe have already made their decision about me, and my fate. I'm going to die. So, if I'm going to die, I'm going to make sure they know how I feel.

"Can I have a drink?" I ask Axe.

"Get her something," he says to Champagne.

Champagne switches into the kitchen, and returns back with a beer. She hands me the beer and sits next to Axe again.

"Let me guess, your favorite drink is Long Island Ice tea," Axe says to me. "I never met you before now, but I remember Brillo telling me that."

*Please wake up Brillo. Please wake up. I need your help now. Please.*

I look at Marcy and Champagne. They have been grooming me for this moment from day one. They are vicious. "When I was more immature, I enjoyed the taste of Long Island Ice Tea." I open the beer and swallow half of it.

"But, like most cheap things in life," I eyeball Champagne and Marcy, "you outgrow them with time."

Marcy and Champagne aren't smiling anymore.

"Answer the question," Axe says to me. "Do you love my brother?"

*Wake up, Brillo. Please.*

"I love Brillo," I say trying to stay still even though my body is trembling. "And, there is nothing Crystal or anybody else can do to change that."

I sit back in the recliner and grin. I'm sipping my beer, until suddenly something is wrapped around my throat. The smell of onions is strong. It's Nita. The beer falls out of my hand, and rolls onto the hardwood floor. I run my finger over the thing on my neck to see what it is. It's a rope.

I look out at Champagne and Marcy, who I spent the last two weeks of my life with. They look heartless and cold. How can anybody be like this? I don't understand.

My breaths are short, and my vision is blurry.

I'm dying.

I'm dying.

# Chapter Thirty-Seven

I'm in a box, under the ground. Marcy, Champagne and Axe drove me here…to my final resting place. I don't know if they thought I was dead when they buried me alive, or if they didn't care. I guess it doesn't matter anyway. I'm here and I'm going to die here.

So can you see now why I had to tell you my entire story? From the beginning to the end? I feel sorry for anybody who runs into Marcy, Champagne and Crystal in their lifetime.

I'm sure by this time tomorrow Marcy, Champagne and Crystal will be on somebody's beach. They'll have fake passports in their possession, and they'll be out of the country. They will return to the states though. They make too much money here to stay away too long. I'm sure of it.

My breath feels like its being pulled from my body now, and I can hardly breathe. I'm going to die. I'm about to die.

"Porsche," I hear somebody scream above the ground. The voice is very faint, but I hear it all the same.

It's Brillo!

"Baby, can you hear me?" He repeats.

I don't have enough energy to scream. My breath is leaving my body more rapidly. Any energy I use will make my life shorter. Oh please, God, let Brillo find me. Please let him save my life. I don't want to die. I want to go to school. I want to be a better person. I want to have a family, and see my children grow up to be the best that they can. I want to make up with my mother, and support her in her sobriety. I want to live. Oh, God I want to live!

"Porsche, don't die on me," Brillo continues to yell above the ground.

My eyes feel lighter now, and suddenly I don't feel scared anymore. I don't hear Brillo either; maybe he gave up, and left me all alone. It doesn't matter anyway, because the bright light I see now is so welcoming, and warm. It feels like I'm surrounded in the love of God.

I feel like I'm floating when suddenly a blast of cool air hits me in the face, and I'm ripped out of the coffin. My body is thrown on the wet grass, and Brillo presses his mouth firmly against mine. He pushes his air into my body repeatedly, until suddenly I feel stronger, and more alive.

When I finally see his face, he lifts me in his right arm, and pulls me to his chest. "I thought I lost you," he tells me into my ear. "I thought I lost you."

"They tried to kill me," I say out of breath. "They blamed me for what happened to you."

"I told you not to trust them bitches," he says kissing me all over on my cheek. "I told you."

"How did you know I was here?" I say trying to breathe clearly.

He looks behind him. Axe is standing there staring at me with serious eyes. My heart drops, because I think he's about to finish me off. I'm shaking so hard now that my teeth are banging into my tongue, and ripping the flesh. My mouth is now bleeding.

"He's not going to hurt you, Porsche," he says to me rubbing my face with his right hand. "I called him when I got up and everybody was gone in the house."

"Why were you sleeping so long?"

"That bitch drugged me last night," Brillo says. "The bitch Marcy."

"I knew it," I say.

"So when I got up and everyone was gone, I called Axe. He told me he was on his way back, and had just left you to die. He told me where you were. I had one of the doctors bring me here, so I could meet Axe to find out where you were. You see, I came back for you. I saved your life," he winks. "We should be even now," he smiles at me.

I love his smile.

"What about Marcy and them?" I ask him. "Did they get away with Axe's money?"

"They got it," Brillo says. "But, you don't have to worry about them, Porsche. Because sooner or later they gonna get what they deserve. I bet money on that."

His statement sounded like a promise instead of a prediction.

Shit may have gotten serious now.

LOVE THE ADVENTURES OF
THE DRUNK & HOT GIRLS?
STAY TUNED FOR THE NEXT SERIES:

*Drunk & Hot Girls*

# THE MEMORIAL DAY WEEKEND MASSACRE

They never wanted the power,
but they stepped to the throne
PRETTY
KINGS
T. STYLES
NATIONAL BEST SELLING AUTHOR OF *RAUNCHY*

THE CARTEL PUBLICATIONS
"We Reign Supreme"

CARTEL PUBLICATIONS
PRESENTS

**The Cartel Collection**
**Established in January 2008**
**We're growing stronger by the month!!!**
**www.thecartelpublications.com**

Cartel Publications Order Form
Inmates ONLY get novels for $10.00 per book!

| ***Titles*** | ***Fee*** |
|---|---|
| Shyt List | $15.00 |
| Shyt List 2 | $15.00 |
| Pitbulls In A Skirt | $15.00 |
| Pitbulls In A Skirt 2 | $15.00 |
| Pitbulls In A Skirt 3 | $15.00 |
| Victoria's Secret | $15.00 |
| Poison | $15.00 |
| Poison 2 | $15.00 |
| Hell Razor Honeys | $15.00 |
| Hell Razor Honeys 2 | $15.00 |
| A Hustler's Son 2 | $15.00 |
| Black And Ugly As Ever | $15.00 |
| Year of The Crack Mom | $15.00 |
| The Face That Launched a Thousand Bullets | $15.00 |
| The Unusual Suspects | $15.00 |
| Miss Wayne & The Queens of DC | $15.00 |
| Year of The Crack Mom | $15.00 |
| Familia Divided | $15.00 |
| Shyt List III | $15.00 |
| Shyt List IV | $15.00 |
| Raunchy | $15.00 |
| Raunchy 2 | $15.00 |
| Raunchy 3 | $15.00 |
| Reversed | $15.00 |
| Quita's Dayscare Center | $15.00 |
| Quita's Dayscare Center 2 | $15.00 |
| Shyt List V | $15.00 |
| Deadheads | $15.00 |
| Pretty Kings | $15.00 |
| Drunk & Hot Girls | $15.00 |

***Please add $4.00 per book for shipping and handling.***
The Cartel Publications * P.O. Box 486 * Owings Mills * MD * 21117

Name: ____________________

Address: ____________________

City/State: ____________________

Contact # & Email: ____________________

***Please allow 5-7 business days for delivery. The Cartel is not responsible for prison orders rejected.***

22757158R00136

Made in the USA
Lexington, KY
12 May 2013

[9]